The Cowboy Christmas Charm

CIARA KNIGHT

Reader Letter

Dear Reader,

I hope you enjoy this special Christmas story that takes you into the life of Francine Mckinnie Hunt great, great, great, great grandaughter from Love on the Sound.

This idea came to me when I asked my newsletter followers what they wanted most for this holiday, a reunion with the McKinnie Sisters or a new contemporary story. It was split down the middle. Being the reader pleaser I am, I had to write something for both votes.

I hope this story fills your hearts with the spirit of Christmas and the legend of the Cowboy Christmas Charm.

Sincerely,
Ciara

Chapter One

CHURCH BELLS RANG, echoing the announcement of Saige McKinnie and Thomas MacLaine's upcoming nuptials as if angels sang the news to the world. Angels like her mother.

The chimes nudged Saige's pulse into an anxious pitter-pat. She took a deep breath, smoothed the satin layers, and eyed herself in the long bridal suite mirror.

The tiara's diamonds sparkled in the light as if highlighting her already noticeable fire-red hair. Hair like her mother's. "Mama, I wish you were here."

A tear pooled in the corner of her eye, but she stuck to her vow never to cry again since she'd left her hometown a decade ago.

She cleared her throat and swished left then right, admiring the Italian lace–lined decolletage and the tiny pearls shimmering in the light. White material fitted in the mermaid style piled into a shiny silk pool at her feet.

The potpourri on the table smelled of cinnamon and spice. The familiar aroma brought a rush of memories galloping in from her childhood. A childhood full of laughter and riding horses and feeling loved, but the absence of her mother had stolen her youth along with her father's heart.

A knock on the door drew her from her reflection to discover Thomas—her future—standing inside the door holding a folder.

She tried to duck behind the mirror, but the tulle veil caught on the edge of the couch, so she backstepped. "What're you doing? It's bad luck to see your bride before the wedding."

He quirked a blond brow at her. "Since when do you subscribe to nonsense and superstitions?"

"It's my wedding day. I'm a girl."

He shrugged. "I didn't think you were the sentimental type."

She fluffed her dress and fluttered her lashes. "What do you think?

He plopped the folder down on the mahogany wood coffee table. "You look nice."

"Nice?" she screeched more than asked.

He looked at her, confusion in his eyes. "What would you like me to say?"

"I don't know, but more than nice." Her wedding day high drifted below the clouds, and she eyed the folder. "I think business can wait a few days."

The distant sound of cars buzzing by outside reminded her there were people waiting for them to walk down the aisle.

"You, the woman who ordered a phone and a laptop twenty minutes after you woke from an emergency appendectomy? The woman who flew to Dubai to close a business deal instead of attending her cousin's wedding? The woman who hasn't taken a day off since I met her?"

She shrank from the conversation, not wanting to hear more. "Enough. I get it."

He squeezed her hand. "That's what I like about you."

"That I'm a workaholic with no heart? Thanks."

He opened his mouth, but she decided to change the subject. "What's in the folder?"

"Prenup. Need to sign it before we seal this deal."

The three-inch Jimmy Choo's wobbled under her. "Prenup?"

"Of course. We need to finalize the details of our arrangement." He slipped a pen from his jacket.

"Arrangement?" Her voice cracked, but she opened the folder as if to make sure this wasn't some joke. "That's how you see our marriage?"

"Don't you? We've dated four years, have been engaged for two. We'll remain newlyweds for three and then have two children one year apart, hire a nanny to raise them until they attend boarding school—"

"Boarding school?" She sucked in a quick, stinging breath. Visions of her father sending his secretary to watch her in the school play, packages sent for Christmas in lieu of going home. She stood there and looked at the man she'd thought she'd spend the rest of her life with, but when his words flashed her next fifty years in front of her, doubt covered her like a dark cloud on a rugged mountaintop.

She asked the one thing she needed to know before she could sign. "Do you love me?"

"What?" he asked, his voice dipping to his corporate tone.

"It's a simple question." She picked up the paper and eyed the legal jargon. "Do you love me?"

"Yes. I said those words to you yesterday before you insisted on staying in the hotel suite instead of my apartment."

His apartment, not *theirs*. "I'm not talking about words. I'm talking about how you feel. Do you look at me standing here in this wedding dress and feel an excitement in your gut? Are you ready to rush down the aisle so that we can spend the rest of our lives together? Are you counting the moments until we make love, sealing our vows tonight?"

"What's gotten into you? Where's my Sensible Saige?" He eyed the terms and then chuckled. "Are you not happy with the details?" He pulled the pen top off and scratched through a line. "It's a standard prenup, but we can change it."

"Terms, documents, agreements. Do you hear yourself? We're not signing a corporate contract. We're starting our lives together. What if I don't want to send our kids to boarding school?"

His face was more blank than his heart. He unbuttoned his tuxedo, swiped the tails back, and rested his hands on his hips. "Then we'll keep the nanny, but our children will need to be educated by the right people. They need to attend elite boarding schools if we're to continue growing our empire."

Empire? "That's all this is to you. A business deal." Her insides swished and swirled with thoughts she didn't want to face. "Marriage should be about love and building something. I want what my parents had all those years ago. I can't sign that." Her words slipped from her mouth as easily as the paper slipped through her fingers and floated to the floor.

"This is nonnegotiable. Every arrangement needs a contract. It's smart business." His voice boomed in the small space.

The same reason she'd dated Thomas was the same reason

she couldn't accept his terms now. He was strong, dependable, a good man, but with a distant heart. She took both his hands in hers and willed him to listen. "Thomas, marriage should be more than a contract."

He blinked at her and then stepped back, his hands wilting from her grasp. She twisted her engagement ring, pulled it off, and held it out to him.

A car horn blew outside, wind whipped through the screens with a whistle, and the heater cut on and blew warm air over her cold heart.

He cleared his throat but took the ring. "I thought we were in sync. Had everything planned out."

Saige's heart thumped at a slow but pounding pace. "That's the problem. I need more than a plan. I need…"

"What your parents had?" he asked, his gaze traveling to the floor, then back to her face.

"I don't know, but I know it isn't this."

He eyed the door and then her, his face tightened with emotion. "So that's it? We have all these guests here waiting for us to walk down the aisle, and you're walking away?"

"Unless you can tell me you love me so much it hurts, that you want to be my husband more than anything else in the world. That even if we didn't have kids, or corporations, or contracts, you would still want me." A bridal bouquet–sized lump lodged in her throat. Her breath caught between willing him to sweep her off her feet or walk out of her life.

He slipped the ring and his pen into his pocket and walked out of her life.

Out of her life.

She faced the mirror once more to see herself in her wedding dress designed by the best and brightest. The dress no one would ever see. No, not a dress. A costume. A real dress would be her mother's gown, which probably still sat tucked away under her bed at the ranch.

The door creaked open, and her father peered inside. "Sounds like the wedding's off."

Saige spun in a white whirl, ready to be berated by her father's disappointment. "I couldn't do it. He brought a prenup on the morning of our wedding. This was never more than a business arrangement. No love, no passion, no...I don't know. Something. Something more than a business deal and a handshake." The emotion of it all bubbled and brewed and battled its way up from her chest and out of her mouth.

He entered the room with his normal take-charge presence but with a hint of softness she hadn't seen in years. Not since her mother had died. "You'll come through this. You're more bull than bunny."

His words sucker-slapped her across her perfectly painted face. Saige bent over, grasping the marble countertop of the vanity, dusted with pale-pink blush residue. Her lungs tightened with shock and sadness. "You're right. And I got myself into this. They always say daughters go for men like their fathers," she mumbled under her breath.

"You've got an amazing career. Why do you need a man?" He stepped into the room, took a peppermint from the crystal dish, and popped it into his mouth. "Love can be a distraction."

The Christmas tree–colored walls closed in around her. "Do you miss her at all?" Her bitterness tasted sour on her tongue.

His blank affect twitched with warning. "Your mother has

been gone for years. It's time to let her go. She was weak." His voice cracked under a decade of pain he'd never faced. They'd fled her family ranch, never to return. He'd shut his heart off, and she'd buried herself in work to make him happy. Somewhere, at some point, she'd buried herself so deep she couldn't see the light.

Saige walked up behind him and dared to touch a hand to his shoulder. "She didn't leave us. Cancer took her."

"She should've fought harder." He straightened and adjusted his tie in the mirror, reflecting the man he'd become the day after his wife had died. The loss had destroyed him.

"Your decision not to go through with the wedding will cause some bad publicity, but you'll handle it. You're more like me. I think it's time to talk about making you partner. Of course, you'll need to change your last name back to Blakely. No matter how much you try, you're not like her. And that's a good thing. You're stronger and would never fall to sickness or let love get in your way."

"I changed my name to Mom's maiden name so that I wouldn't be known as your daughter. I fought hard for my position, and no one can say I got there because I carried the Blakely last name."

He lifted his chin. "You've proven yourself, so you can change it back," he said in a tone that told her to back off for now and pick up the fight later.

Her father waltzed over to the mirror and ran his finger over his brow as if to order each hair into proper position like he ordered everyone around him.

That was Thomas. She'd fallen into the cliché of marrying a man like her father. Cold, distant, all deals and work but no passion. They weren't bad men. They donated to charities, paid their employees well, but they kept their hearts closed off from possibilities. "I've taken care of the attendees and explained how you realized that you had more to do in your life before you settled down. No one was surprised. Like me, they didn't understand this farce."

"Farce? I loved him until..." She eyed the paper she couldn't sign. Not because she cared about the idea of not taking money from him if they ever divorced, but because it was just another contract between them. She wanted more out of marriage than a business arrangement.

He cupped her cheek and looked into her eyes as if to say the most profound words to soothe her pain. "Did you?" Her father squeezed her shoulders. "You're not a little girl anymore. Those childhood fantasies of happily ever after don't exist in real life."

Saige saw it, the truth in his words. Somewhere, she'd gone down a different path than she'd vowed as a little girl. Where had things gone wrong? "I miss her."

He went to the window, looked out, and spoke in a distant tone. "She's gone, and she'll never come back. She'll never have the life you have now." He spun on his heels and strutted from the bridal room, leaving Saige alone.

Alone.

When was the last time she'd laughed or found real joy in life? She wrapped her arms around herself and sighed. The MH ranch. Maybe it was time to go home and face what her father never could, reconnect with her mother and the McKinnie family. The stories and legends she'd grown up on about the seven sisters and their great adventures. She could ride horses instead of taxis, smell fresh air instead of pollution, snuggle by a roaring wood fire instead of a gas-lit flame.

She removed her dress and tossed it on the velvet couch, grabbed her keys, the envelope with the two thousand dollars of tip money she'd planned to give to the staff after the wedding, and snuck out the back door.

Bitter wind beat at her thin sweater–covered arms. Pipe organ Christmas music sounded from inside the church. Gray skies made her feel like nothing waited for her beyond business and lonely nights. She knew she couldn't disappear without a word, so she texted her father.

You're right. I'm nothing like mother, but unlike you, I want to be. I'm going far from here to figure out who I am. I love you, but I want more out of my life than a contract.

He responded by the time she reached the parking lot and spotted her lone car.

Take a few days. I'll see you at the office on Monday.

No, he wouldn't, but she needed distance before she would tell him she had no plans of returning until she reconnected with her mother and figured out what she wanted out of life beyond work.

Inside her car, she cranked up the heat and eyed the workmen installing Christmas lights on the street corner. Despite the fact that it was the first day of December, they were working like the holiday was fast approaching instead of looming ahead, taunting her with the truth. The truth that she had no one to celebrate the holidays with.

Since she had no desire to fly off to the tropics alone. She gripped the leather steering wheel and rested her head against it.

She wanted to feel closer to her mother, to remember the

happier times of her life. The last time she felt alive and happy. To channel the woman she wanted to be, not this person she'd become. When had everything turned so wrong in her life?

The MH ranch. It had been a decade since Saige had gone all the way out to her mother's family home. She'd hired her cousin to run it as a rental for the last five years.

The place had been her refuge as a child. Beautiful scenery and the only place her parents ever went that they didn't fight. Probably because it was in the middle of nowhere and since there was no cell service and the snow took out the phone lines, often her father couldn't work. They'd all be happy if only for a week or two at a time.

Saige hadn't been back since her mother died. The night of her funeral, her father had packed Saige up and they left, never to return. Not that she'd argued, since there was nothing left for her in that town after her mother's death, and Trevor... She hadn't thought of that name since that day, and she wouldn't think of him now. An insignificant memory from her past.

She texted her cousin to let him know she'd be heading out there and started her car. She needed to get a move on if she wanted to make it before she got caught in a winter storm. A common occurrence this time of year.

The idea of seeing the beautiful ranch her great-great-great-great-grandmother and grandfather had built in the 1870s warmed her insides, despite the coldness of rejection still taking up residence. If she had to be alone for the holidays, at least she'd feel close to her mother again. And hopefully figure out why she'd turned to money and success instead of family and friends.

❄

The Hummer limo hung a right onto a snowy path, jostling the members of the Billionaire Boys Club into each other. Crystal glasses clinked along with Colt's ridiculous cowboy boots and hat the men made him wear as an initiation into their elite group.

He almost felt as ridiculous as the time his father dressed him in a tuxedo at the age of six to stand by his side as he made some big announcement at the Whitmore Company Christmas party. He couldn't remember the details, but if they were like all the others, his father had taken over some other smaller company to add to his empire. Colt often pictured his old man with a battle axe and had nicknamed him King Whitmore, Conqueror of Businesses.

The Hummer slowed. Colt eyed the snow oasis of tall pines and rugged mountains in the distance. He wasn't in Los Angeles or Chicago anymore. He'd traded in big city for big adventure. A place far from boardrooms and boredom.

The men held up their lowballs with a grunt, then knocked their whiskey back. He should've known by the title of the group that this adventure would be more frat party and less escapism.

Lucas, one of the BBC minions, cleared his voice and pounded on his chest. "Hear ye, hear ye. Billionaire Bad Boy Colt Whitmore cares more about partying and womanizing than running his father's global empire. A man born with a silver Mercedes in his mouth is caught with a sheik's wife in his arms."

Colt snatched the paper, balled it up, and tossed it on the ground but then couldn't handle the mess and picked it up, tucking it into the corner. "Enough. I'm here to get away from all that."

Colt scanned the inviting scenery once more. White light streaked through parted, puffy clouds dancing in a crystal sky, casting a shadow from the large two-story home onto the shimmering white ground. Weather had beaten down the home the way Colt had been worn down by his life choices. Choices he didn't regret yet paid the price for anyway.

"Don't think anyone will think to look for you here," the president of the minions announced.

Lucas turned and eyed the world outside. "What a dump."

He wasn't wrong. The house stood in the foreground with weathered posts, broken front porch railing, and a brittle roof Colt feared might cave in from the weight of the snow. But he could imagine the charm of living in such a place, with flower boxes dotting the railing of the wraparound porch during the spring, a large Christmas tree in the front window during the winter, and fresh lemonade on a summer afternoon while watching little ones playing in the front pasture. A great change from the hustle of the big city he'd left behind. The big life he'd left behind. But he didn't belong here either.

"It's a night to blow off steam and party. A roof and some drinks are all we need," the president of this rich and ridiculous group said.

"As long as we don't get bitten by a rat or something," a minion mumbled.

What was Colt thinking, joining a pompous group filled with rich playboys who had no focus? Sure, he'd had fun on the slopes earlier, but the distraction hadn't lasted any longer than a minute after he removed his skies. Deep down, he knew why. He was tired of fighting everyone's opinion of him, so he tried to embrace it. The lazy, partying, useless son.

How could anyone be happy when they had no purpose in life? And Colt had no purpose. Not unless he was ready to take his inherited right to stand at the feet of his mighty father on the corporate throne.

Colt unfurled his long legs and found the fresh air welcoming. A chill tapped at the end of his nose, but the quiet of the mountains warmed his insides. "Not so bad."

Joe smacked him on the back. "Anything's better than facing dear ol' dad, Worthless Whitmore."

Colt tensed at the nickname he'd never live down. At least here, he only had seven other guys to remind him of his epic, public embarrassment and the label of a useless, lazy, and disappointing son. Seven men who'd sworn brotherly love and pounded on their chests all day, yet he only remembered two names. One, Lucas, because he spent most of the day talking about his conquests with the ladies yet found rejection every time he made a pass at one.

And Joe, the man who burped and announced how great he was and how much he was worth anytime he could fit it into conversation. "I should've booked us. I know all the right people."

To keep himself from opening his bitter trap to remind Joe he only knew the people his parents knew and could only afford what his allowance allowed, Colt took a few steps to peek around the edge of the house at the amazing view. He enjoyed the sound of crushing snow under his boots, despite the others griping about it being cold and damp.

The driver unloaded and took their bags into the house, where they would be spending the next few days. Maybe there were horses to ride or something around here. The idea of sitting inside the house with these men for seventy-two hours didn't appeal to Colt. He'd spent the last decade in a fog with no purpose but pleasing his father, an unattainable goal.

"Should be fully stocked," the president announced and hoofed it up the rickety steps into the house, where a warm and cozy parlor welcomed them.

"Did you rent this place on the site I told you to, or is this from DesperateandDesolate.com?" Joe groaned and stomped on the antique wood floors.

The smell of musty grandma furniture mixed with a hint of mold wasn't a welcoming odor, but the old house had charm. Colt followed the others down the main hall but paused at a table covered in old photos. He picked up a picture housed in an antique gold frame, wiped the thick dust from the glass, and studied the family who appeared happy. A little girl and her parents rode horses through an open field covered in dandelions. The woman and girl had striking red hair he'd only seen in the movies. They all looked happy. A family—a real family. Maybe this place housed the elusive miracle, unlike his parents and their lost, loveless marriage.

"We're the brothers, we're the way. We'll never turn our back or sway. We vow to honor one another. Because we are now and forever brothers."

The chanting from the end of the hall spoke of the next round of drinks. Colt returned the picture and joined the others, figuring this was what the weekend was about, forgetting his troubles for a while and embracing what everyone thought of him. A lazy drunken fool with no appreciation for the gifts he'd been given in life. Just because he preferred dating over any faux commitment didn't make him a bad person. It made him smart.

"Hey, check out that view," the man with the oversized cowboy hat called out and flung open the back doors and took a step, falling face-first into the snow.

Colt strutted to the door to discover the back deck only had two boards near the house and four corner posts sticking up out of the ground. If he had his tools, he could build a new deck. He missed working with his hands.

The man popped up without his ridiculous hat. "I'm done. Call the limo back." He shuffled waist-deep to the door, and Colt gave him a hand up.

"Already used that old-fashioned corded contraption on the wall to call since there's no cell service. No flight out until morning, and the company says it's not safe to drive the roads after dark due to the abundance of wildlife in the area and the snow," the president of the group said.

Lucas unloaded a black duffel of hard liquor. "Guess we better party the night away, then. We'll head back to civilization tomorrow."

Colt remained at the door another minute. Civilization? Nope, not ready for that. "I think I'll stick around. Just arrange for the car to come back in a couple days."

Joe downed a shot and hammered his glass against the tile countertop. "You insane? You actually want to stay here?" He squealed like a trapped pig.

The twin brothers gawked at each other. "He's hiding out. No better place to disappear than here."

They weren't wrong. "Listen, I could use a few days of quiet after all the media coverage. Don't worry about me. I don't mind roughing it a little."

"A little? I think I saw an outhouse." Lucas poured another round.

This time, The guy—Colt thought maybe his name was Craig—joined in and raised his glass. "To the BBC," he said in hopes of changing the subject. At least they'd be gone in the morning, and he wouldn't have to look at another person who judged him for his epic public disaster.

He slammed back a strong, chest-warming shot. And for the next ten hours, he indulged. Indulged until he couldn't stand up and passed out. When he woke up, he pulled the straw from his hair and sat up to a spinning room. His head pounded and the odor of the horse or cow or whatever animal made his stomach give him a one-two punch for poisoning himself all night.

He pulled himself up and managed to stumble from a big red barn in time to see the men loading up the limo.

"There he is. Last chance, bro."

Not only did the idea of leaving this place far from civilization not sit well with him, but neither did the copious amounts of alcohol he'd consumed. Maybe it was time to rethink his lifestyle after all. "All good. Staying put."

"Best you did. You don't look like a guy who needs to be in a closed-in space on rough roads right now." Craig tossed a blanket off his shoulders and swung it over the front porch railing before he disappeared into the limo.

Colt waved them off and stumbled up to the front porch, where he collapsed onto the swing, cuddled under the oversized furry blanket, and decided to sleep it off for a while enjoying his peace and quiet.

He zonked out and didn't move until something cold and wet splashed into his face. "Wh-What?" He fell off the swing onto the hard floor with a loud thud before another foul-smelling bit of water hit his face. "What the...?"

He scurried to his feet with fists up, ready to pound one of the men, but spotted a small, red-haired girl with big green eyes and even bigger attitude. "Who the hell are you, and what are you doing squatting at my house?"

Chapter Two

SAIGE DROPPED the bucket and grabbed her granny's old rifle. Her gut clenched tight, but she was less scared and more angry after seeing the inside of her beloved childhood ranch. Good thing the gun wasn't loaded, or she might actually shoot him.

The intruder with a dark hat and flannel button-up cursed and carried on as if she'd thrown cow dung on him instead of water. She wished she would've thought of that.

"You crazy..."

Oh, he wouldn't go there. No way she was backing down from a man who called her crazy, as if she was some hysterical female. Been in too many boardrooms with Neanderthals to take that attitude anymore. *Women were crazy. Men were strong.* And this man standing at over six feet, broad-shouldered and thin waist accentuated by his ridiculous belt buckle, told her he thought of himself as king of the Neanderthals.

He had no right to be mad. She had every right to wake up the scoundrel who had wrecked her place. "What did you do to my house?"

He spit water from his mouth and swiped his sleeve over his lips. "Your house?" The man removed his black cowboy hat and brushed his short hair back. Not that there was too much, since he was a short-and-tight type. Yet he stunk of booze and day-old barn.

"Yes, my house." She pointed the gun at his broad chest.

He took a step forward, large hands splayed out in front of him. "Whoa. Lower that thing. Someone could get hurt, sweetheart."

Oh no he didn't, belittling a woman with unsolicited terms of endearment. Thinking that sexy swagger of his would get anywhere near her libido. "I'm not your sweetheart." She'd met enough bull riders to know this man was all good looks with empty space in his head. Something she'd learned back in high school when she'd been dumped for a buckle bunny by her own sweetheart.

He exhaled a puff of white air, letting her know she'd made her point, and the guy would catch pneumonia standing out here drenched. Fine. She'd get him inside to work. That would warm him up. "Before you go, you're cleaning up that mess. I'm over men like you running off and leaving your messes behind for others to clean up."

A flash of something in his eyes told her she'd hit a nerve. "Listen, some of my friends rented this place."

"Doesn't give you the right to destroy it. I revoke your privilege of being on my property. Now fix my house and get out of here."

The man grinned, a lopsided, I-know-I'm-sexy kind of smile. "Where am I supposed to go?" He scooted closer, calling her bluff.

"Don't care. Not my problem."

He pressed two fingers to the barrel and nudged it out of the way.

She jolted it back at his face. He grabbed the barrel with one hand, yanked it out, pulled her to his chest, and then tossed the gun over the railing. "Someone should teach you some manners. You could've killed me."

His arms locked strong around her. A man. A stranger. She pushed at his chest. "Let go."

"Not until you promise not to shoot me."

She fought and squirmed and would've clocked him a good one to show him who was boss, but her arms were trapped between them. This man was strong. Too strong. Yet, he only held her tight enough to keep her from escaping to grab her weapon. Something told her he held back a real show of strength.

Which ticked her off even more. She was the one in charge. "I said let me go. This is assault."

"No, self-defense. You pointing a gun at a paying guest is the real crime here. Not going to look good on my review." He snickered.

Did he think this was some sort of game? She wiggled to try to free one arm. That was all she needed, and he'd be on his butt. "You probably didn't even chip in for the rental."

He didn't answer her accusation, which confirmed her suspicion that this man was a washed-up rodeo rider with nowhere to go. She'd seen it one too many times.

"Calm yourself. I'll let you go when you relax and promise not to shoot me."

She stilled but wanted to show him brute force was no longer the only way to be the superior species. "The sheriff is a personal friend of the family. I suggest you let go of me, or you'll find yourself in a cell."

He didn't loosen his grip. "One of those types, huh?"

"What type?"

His arms loosened a little but not enough.

"The type that has to call in favors to win the fight."

Oh, his words irked her. Especially knowing the sheriff was no friend of hers. "I can fight my own battles." She knew they were getting nowhere except pressed together in a way she hadn't experienced in years. Sure, she'd been intimate with her now ex, but it was never passionate. It had always been safe, though. That's what she'd wanted—stability, not all passion and fire. Had she made a grave mistake not marrying Thomas? She'd had an "all the feelings" kind of relationship once. A long time ago. Once was enough for one lifetime. There had to be something in between. Safe but exciting. "Fine. I won't shoot you. For now."

He released her, but before he could take a step away, she pressed her hands to his chest and shoved him away before she decided the warmth was welcome in this bitter cold.

Control. She needed to regain it.

She pointed to the snowy front yard where he'd thrown her rifle. "Why'd you do that? That was my granny's gun."

"So? That gives you the right to shoot one of your guests?"

"Guest implies you were invited. I didn't invite you." Saige huffed and traipsed down the steps, shuffled through the snow, and dove in to find the gun. "I bet you weren't the one paying anyway. Looks like you've been sleeping in the barn."

"You're not wearing any gloves. You'll end up with frostbite."

"Better than being bitten by you."

He leaned over the railing, and his brow went from tight concern to playful rise. "Interesting."

"What's that?" She shuffled through the snow until her boot made contact with something hard.

"You thinking about me biting you."

She dove her hands into the icy snow, welcoming the cooling effect on her flushed body. This man riled her up. Not acceptable. "Wouldn't think anything except that I might catch something. Guessing you're full of nothing but ego and STDs." She found the gun and yanked it from the snow, flung it over her shoulder, and marched up the porch.

He turned at an angle as if ready to do battle.

Not wanting to end up back in his arms again for more reasons than she cared to face at the moment, she rested the gun against the porch. "Relax. It's not loaded."

A playful smirk arched at the corners of his mouth, revealing dimples. Ugh, not those. She'd been a sucker once for a man with dimples but had avoided them ever since. The man in front of her was ridiculous and wrong in every way, from his black hat to his impractical boots.

"They were a bet," he grumbled, as if reading her mind. "My buddies, the ones who apparently trashed your place, had me wear these. Didn't think I'd be seeing anyone."

"Where's the rest of your Neandermen?"

"Neandermen?" He leaned his butt against the railing, crossed his arms over his chest, and swung his foot to rest the toe of his boot against the floor. That go-to Stetson commercial kind of pose.

"A man who's still stuck halfway in his ancestral Neanderthal roots."

He laughed, a big, hearty echo through the vastness of the beautiful mountains kind of belly chuckle.

"Back to the point. Where's the rest of you?"

He shrugged. "Gone."

"What do you mean, gone?" she asked, scanning the place for a vehicle but only spotting her own.

"They left early this morning."

"Ditched you, huh?" She snickered. "Not much loyalty with that gang. Come on. I'll make some coffee while you clean up this place, and then you can call a ride."

"Great. I could go for a cup."

"Didn't offer you one. Coffee's for me." She sashayed into the house that had once brought her so much joy, but even now it felt haunted with the memories of what could've been.

Chapter Three

THE WOMAN with the swaying hips and beautiful full lips drew him in like the flicker of a candle—mesmerizing, but if not handled with care, it could start a fire. "You own this place?" he asked.

"Thought we already established that." She looked over her shoulder, her long red hair with a hint of curl at the bottom swaying across her thin back. "Get kicked in the head one too many times by a bull?"

"What makes you think I'm a bull rider?" Not that he minded. The idea of being someone else for the moment sounded perfect.

"*Ex*-bull rider. Ridiculous outfit, horrible friends who leave you stranded, and that stupid I-own-all-women-with-one-sexy-grin attitude."

"You think I have a sexy grin?" He liked that idea. This woman was bold and beautiful and bossy. Nothing like the *bred to bend at his every whim* type he'd been introduced to a hundred times by his stepmother.

"Kind of missed the point. Yep, definitely a washed-up bull rider. Only hear the compliments; never facing the truth."

She shimmied out of her coat and hung it on a hook, then went to work making coffee. The woman had curves in all the right places, held her head high, and moved like a ballet dancer with an ax ready to strike him down. She was an enigma. And he liked figuring out puzzles. "Maybe us ex-bull riders are really sensitive underneath the bravado."

"Sure, so sensitive you can't face the mess you make and run out without cleaning it up."

"What do you mean?"

She filled the coffee pot full of water with one hand and pointed to the room behind him with the other. "Get to work."

Something told him that she wasn't talking about the physical mess. There was a crumb to a bigger story and he wanted to follow it, but when he turned to find the room with a busted lamp, stains on the rug, and empty bottles of booze scattered around, conviction took hold. He couldn't stand disorder, and the sight of it all compelled him to take action. He needed to make this right.

When they'd rented this place, they hadn't thought of it as someone's home. Maybe the papers were right about him. Maybe he was spoiled and unfeeling. Maybe this was an opportunity to rehab from playboy to purpose.

"Not going to clean itself."

"Yes, ma'am," he said, showing respect instead of sounding arrogant. At least he hoped.

She didn't criticize his word choice, so he guessed it was fine. He went to work, and boy was it a job. He liked his now ex-friends even less after an hour of bending and picking things up with a sour belly, a headache, and having to smell that delicious eye-opening coffee aroma without a sip to give him some much-needed energy.

He righted the lamp and made a mental note to order a new one and have it shipped when he returned home. Not that he had any intention of returning home, but despite the payoff in his account to get out of town, he had no idea where he wanted to go. Not to mention he didn't want to take a dime of his father's money. He'd been living off his own savings, but with the extravagant lifestyle of the Billionaire Boys Club, he guessed his savings was near depleted after only a week. What would it be like to live without a constant flow of cash at his disposal? To be a man without means and have to work to earn his way in the world.

"Here." A perfectly manicured hand held out something red and stomach-churning, and then another cup followed, filled to the brim with coffee. "Hangover relief, ranch-style, and a cup of joe for energy."

"Thanks." He collapsed into the recliner that tipped back too far, and he spilled a drop of the tomatoey liquid onto his shirt. Great. This day kept improving.

"Don't think about it. Just down it."

He held his breath and chugged the lowball glass of something rich, spicy, and gag-inducing. After he gulped it down, he retched then recovered. "Sorry."

"No reason to apologize. That's what it does. Makes you almost get sick, and then everything gets coated with whatever magic powers it possesses. My granny taught me how to make it." She smiled at the mention of her grandmother, and it warmed his insides. Or was that the concoction? After all, he was an unfeeling womanizer.

"Back in your party days, huh?"

"Nope. Granny had a certain way about her. She was old-school and said a woman needed to know how to woo and control a man without him even knowing she's doing it."

"You trying to woo me?" He winked, but based on her tight-lipped expression, he retreated from his normal flirtations. "Right. Thanks."

"No need to thank me. Figured if I wanted this entire house cleaned, I needed to give you some energy. Looks like you can't handle your liquor any more than the rest of the bull riders I've known."

"Dated them, huh?"

"I'm no buckle bunny," she hissed in warning.

He held up his hands, because for once in his life, he didn't know the right thing to say to a woman. Instead, he followed her pointer finger to the dining room, where he discovered his friends were Neanderthals like she'd accused them of, because no gentleman would ever leave a bra hanging from a buckhorn chandelier. He had no desire to know where that bra came from, considering there were only men here last night. Then he realized what she thought. "We didn't have some bachelor party or escorts here."

She tapped her foot, and the way her head tilted to the side, he knew she didn't believe him. Why should she? The circumstantial evidence sealed his fate by the judge and jury watching him work.

By the time he cleaned up the puke, removed the bra, and cleaned the dishes, throwing out the ones that were broken, he thought he'd get a reprieve.

"There. All done."

He placed his hands on his lower back and stretched out the kinks with a pop or two and then spotted her at the stairs.

"Just getting started."

A part of him wanted to throw in the towel and tell her he'd hire someone to clean the place, but since she already had a poor view of his work ethic and making messes he didn't clean up, he decided to see this through. Maybe he'd build some character through this process. Lord knew he needed some help in that department. He either needed to be stone cold for his father's respect or devoted and doting like his mother. Unfortunately, he was neither. Never did fit in with either parent. His brother, on the other hand, was born to be his father's minion. All work and no questions or defiance. And his baby sister, well, she was the most loveable creature on earth. One would think she was from his parents, but no, she was the product of his family-wrecking stepmother.

Colt climbed the stairs and didn't even make it to one of the bedrooms before seeing evidence of another overindulgence on the carpet runner. Shame filled him. This house really was trashed.

To his surprise, she came up with her own bucket full of supplies. "I'll get to work in the master."

"You don't have to do that. My boys made the mess. I'll clean it up." He dropped to his knees, dipped the brush in water, and tended to the stain.

She eyed him with a disapproving swish of her lips. "No, not like that." She knelt by him, grabbed his hand holding the brush, dipped it in the bucket, and scrubbed the carpet. Her tiny fingers were strong but soft. "You need more water to get that stain out."

Her touch sent a heat wave up his arm he hadn't antici-pated, or was that his hangover? His pulse ta-tapped faster, and his breath came shorter. The touch of a woman always stirred him up inside, but this was different. Maybe it was because he knew this woman had no interest in him other than manual labor. Most women would've forgone the judgment and raced him into their bed.

Maybe his father hadn't been entirely wrong. He'd been entertaining the wrong type of women. His father never cared but had warned him not to get caught. A philosophy he guessed served both his marriages well over the years. Colt wanted more than the one-night stands, but marriage was a farce. He wanted to know more about this woman in front of him down on her hands and knees working, but he figured if he tried anything, she'd throw him out or shoot him.

Chapter Four

THE SUN SET before the work was done, and Saige realized the fatal error in her anger. No way he'd be able to get a ride out of here at this hour. Never a good idea to traverse those winding, cliffside roads at night during winter, not to mention the rogue animals running out in front of the vehicle.

She had to give this man credit. Most bucking bronco types would've walked out with a backhand wave, leaving her with the mess to clean up. One rodeo star in particular had a gift for that. A man she had refused to think of since the last time she'd been at this house.

But now that she stood in the master bedroom, where she'd cried on more than one occasion in her mother's arms, haunting memories of that time in her life came flooding in. Not just of her mother but of her old life with her ex. Probably because a more handsome version of him stood nearby. That wasn't what she was here for, though. She'd come back to reconnect with the McKinnie women, not some loser ex. "You're kind of tall for a bull rider. You still riding?"

He pulled the sheet from the bed and tossed it in the wash

pile. That dark eyebrow rose, drawing her attention to his sapphire eyes. She was a sucker for baby blues and dark hair. Some might say it had been her type. Yet, Thomas, her ex-fiancé, had light hair and brown eyes.

"Bull riding?" She nudged him, realizing that hangover and exhaustion were fogging his brain.

"I can safely say I'm not riding any bulls now or in my future." He chuckled as if there was more to that story. Of course there would be. All his kind had stories of conquests, bulls, and booze.

"What's next for you, then? Plan to drink your troubles away?" She grabbed the other side of the fitted sheet he wrestled with and helped him strip the bedding.

"Sounds like a solid plan," he said with a wink, "or maybe it's time for me to grow up and give a care."

"Really?" Her turn to raise a brow and point her lie radar at him.

He balled up the sheet and rounded the bed to stand a foot from her, only the bedding between them. His eyelids lowered and his mouth went slack. "I guess you're right. I'm not the hardworking type, or so I've been told."

This man had to be six to eight inches taller than her, his shoulders mountain sized yet not overly bulky. Sweat dotted his temple, probably excreting out the alcohol. Yet, standing alone in this bedroom with him, she didn't feel threatened or judged or dismissed.

She shook off the feeling, took the sheets, and tossed them in the pile they'd started, to put some distance between them. Her breath stuttered but then came more natural, making her realize space would be a good idea. A woman who'd just failed to make it to the altar meant dangerous and wayward emotions.

Things popped into her head like one-night stands and fling-forgetting kind of vacations. She scooped up the sheets and headed to the laundry room. "You can sleep in the downstairs room off the kitchen."

"Wait, what?" He followed her, close enough to cause her feet and pulse to quicken. "Not a good idea." His voice came deep and disturbed, causing a shiver to run up her spine.

Saige dropped the bedding into the laundry room, not daring to enter the small space with him. Too close. Too small for a broken heart. A heart that hadn't beat like this in years. Not when she dated reliable and dependable Thomas. Not since—oh dear Lord, she couldn't be that girl anymore. Not the one who went for bad boys. Bad boys who broke hearts and didn't care. She sucked in a quick breath and straightened, pointing her finger down the hall. "Not done. Two more rooms. Not to mention the kitchen needs to be scrubbed from top to bottom."

He ran a hand through his short hair, and she could imagine it a touch longer, wilder, untamed. She swallowed hard.

"I'll keep working and then call a car." Heat erupted in his eyes, but he turned away and headed for the stairs.

She passed a photo of her mother hanging on the wall as if she stood by in judgment. The McKinnies would've never turned out a man down on his luck. Not in the snow, not anytime. They were good people. The kind of people she wanted to be.

"No one's going to come out here at night. Besides, you can put that cell phone away. Part of the charm of this place is no service. No internet, no cell, no people." Saige headed down the stairs, putting more space between her and the beautiful cowboy. Anger didn't begin to describe how she felt at this moment. She'd spent all those years molding the life she wanted, only to have it implode around her. Where had she gone wrong?

Steps sounded behind her like a trotting horse. She quickened her pace to the kitchen. "Guess we need to eat something and then head to bed." Her voice pitched higher on the word bed. She cleared her throat and refused to look at him. "So we can start early and get you out of here and on with your life."

"On with my life, right." He collapsed into a seat on the other side of the island.

She relaxed a little with a barrier between them. "Not excited to get back to it?"

"Not even a bit." He dropped his head into his hands as if unable to face the world any longer.

A part of her was drawn to comfort him. Another part screamed for her to run into the snow and spend the night in the ice. Frostbite would be safer than sexy and sensitive.

Eggs. Maybe she could make eggs. She'd seen it done by her cook before or at a restaurant. Not that cooking had ever been on her agenda. She opened the refrigerator that housed the few items she'd picked up from the grocery in town, along with the rest that she guessed had been fully stocked by her cousin before these guests had arrived. Guests being a strong word. "How do you like your eggs?"

"You're offering to make me dinner?" He looked up at her as if she'd offered him a five-course meal.

"Girl's gotta eat. And not dinner. Just eggs." She set the Styrofoam case down on the counter and grabbed her granny's old skillet. The one she had used to make sizzling meats and eggs and potatoes and anything else delicious. Saige could almost smell Grandma McKinnie's food that reminded her of happy times. Times before her mother passed, before Traitor Trevor broke her heart, before she'd left this place with plans never to return.

Shoving away the memories, she cracked an egg and dropped it into the pan. Along with a few eggshells. She should've learned to cook when Granny had asked, but she'd always been too busy tending the horses or riding or working the land.

"Need some help?" Colt approached. "I kind of prefer non-crunchy eggs. Why don't you have a seat and I'll whip us up something." His hand covered hers on the spatula, causing more heat than the open flame of the stove. He recoiled as if her hand seared him.

She set the utensil down and gave him space. "Cooking isn't really in my skill set."

"What is your skill set?" The man moved with the grace and power of one of those Cirque du Soleil acrobats around the kitchen.

She averted her gaze to the serene mountains barely visible in the diminishing light. "Conquering and alienating." The words weighed so heavy she couldn't stand another second. The stool squeaked as she turned to face him, only to discover his mouth open.

He recovered with a wicked grin, complete with distracting dimples. "I doubt that."

"Don't let my size fool you. I'm ruthless. Trust me. I have been for a long time."

The way his grin moved from weak to wicked shot warnings through her.

"Stop that."

"What?" He returned his attention to cooking.

"I know that look. A guy likes a challenge, and I'm not interested in being anyone's game."

He turned off the burner and scooped the eggs onto plates, handed one to her along with a fork, and leaned over the counter, over her. "I'm direct. Don't have to play games."

His deep voice echoed through the room to her heart, but she closed it off and countered, "Everyone plays games."

Chapter Five

SAIGE LIT A FIRE LIKE A PRO, a skill Colt didn't possess but decided to add to his list of things to learn with all his free time. He watched as she stood by the flames in what appeared to be deep thought.

A blueish tone shone outside the back doors with a flurry of snow drifting to the ground. Silence filled the room except for a pop of a log in the fire. After a few moments, she looked up at him with such pain in her eyes he longed to pull her into his arms and chase the gloom away. The way he had with his little sister Abbey whenever she'd skin her knee. He missed that little munchkin, but he wasn't ready to head home.

Saige wasn't his sister, though. She was a beautiful, strong but wounded type. Comforting her would be a bad idea because he only knew one way of soothing a woman, and she wasn't the type. And he wasn't capable of anything else. The one trait he couldn't deny he inherited from his father.

"What's on your mind?" he asked, trying to make polite conversation to help her relax. The woman was wound so tight, he thought she might explode at any moment.

She blinked at him, then studied the fire as if it held a secret meaning. Her hair shifted, covering her face, and he wanted to brush it out of the way to see her expression but kept his distance.

"Memories." She sat down in the other chair facing the fire. "My mother. She passed away here a decade ago. I was thinking about the charm she gave me the day before she died. A family heirloom."

"Where is it?" Colt asked, but her lips pressed together and she turned to the outside world instead of to him.

He shifted in the recliner. "I didn't mean to pry. Just making small talk, getting to know you." Something he was trying on since he'd never talked much to the ladies he dated.

The heater kicked on, the clatter drawing her attention to the vent, but only long enough for her to inhale a deep breath then look at him with a stern expression. "No need. You won't be here long enough, and I don't need to get to know someone like you."

Great, she'd seen the papers. All day, he'd thought he'd escaped the drama and gossip but he hadn't. Fine, let her judge him.

She fled the room without another word. Footsteps pounded the ceiling overhead, and then the creak of the bed told him she'd settled into a bedroom upstairs.

Nervous energy polluted with anger set him off. Unable to sit still, he attacked the mess in the kitchen and didn't stop until the stove and countertops were spotless, the inside of the oven scraped free of food debris and scrubbed, floors swept and mopped, main room windows streak-free, and the wood paneling in the dining room wiped down.

He moved to the main room to dust, but fatigue overruled

his cleaning OCD and an ache between his shoulder blades caused him to take a break. At the sight of some old photo albums, he paused and set his rag aside. After a quick glance at the hallway, he snagged a few of the old-fashioned photo books and collapsed into the rocker.

Inside, he discovered pictures of a little Saige with people he assumed were her parents and grandparents, riding horses, roasting marshmallows by the fire, mending fences, and shooting.

Something inside him snapped with realization. He wanted that. A real family with real memories, not the expensive ones his father bought with big trips where they all went their separate ways. But he'd never have that because he wasn't the monogamous family type. Too much of his father ran through his veins.

That woman upstairs with the corporate look, expensive snow boots, perfect hair and eyes appeared so different than the little girl in the photos. But the way she'd wielded that shotgun with hip out and chin up showed she still had the same determination and sass today she'd had in childhood.

He rocked, eyeing the moon and stars in the night sky through the window. He'd always wanted to camp under the night sky somewhere fresh and open, but there were no tents—only offices—in his childhood.

The clock on the mantel ticked away, soothing him with its rhythm. When was the last time he'd crawled into an actual bed and fallen asleep? He'd been like Abbey as a toddler when she'd crawl until she passed out.

Tick. Tick. Tick. Tick.

If Abbey were here, she'd call Saige a unicorn. And he'd have to agree. He snickered at the memory of his little sister sitting at the tea set with him, explaining that a unicorn was a magical creature that only the truly blessed would ever get a chance to see. Saige McKinnie would fit that discerption in his book. The woman upstairs possessed beauty, power, and intelligence. Nothing like the flings of his past or the arrangement with the perfect wife on paper. One that would stay at his side and raise his father's company to a new level. A woman who shopped, played tennis, trained in the art of polite conversation and how to spend money to be part of the elite crowd, all the time having flings on the side. None of that appealed to him. He had no desire for that life, even if it meant not seeing his baby sister.

He'd never meant to embarrass anyone, but he never could find the drive to focus during business meetings and luncheons and banquets. He tried to be the good employee—the good son —but his heart wasn't in it, if he had a heart at all. God knew he had tried.

Tick. Tick. Tick. Tick.

His arms relaxed and he sank into the chair, hoping for some shut-eye, but he knew sleep would never come because insomnia took hold the night his father told him he was no better than an embarrassment to the family.

Yet, his body relaxed in the old, faded cloth recliner, in the old living room, with the old wood mantel fireplace, in the old house with old, good memories. The kind Colt wished he had.

Before he could finish that thought, he swore he smelled coffee. A good, strong brew.

"Good morning. Told you to sleep in the bedroom off the kitchen. Didn't have to sleep here."

He opened his eyes to a beautiful red-haired, green-eyed creature and thought if this was a dream, he didn't want to wake up. But when his memory caught up with his vision, the reality made him smile.

"Whatcha grinning at?" She shoved a coffee at him. "Drink up. We have work to finish."

He took the warm mug and eyed it for a moment, sniffing the brown liquid.

"It's safe. I learned to make coffee when I could reach the pot. Workers on a ranch need coffee. I grew up drinking it." Saige turned and headed for the kitchen. Her swaying hips made him want to follow her, but the coffee would have to do for now.

"Guess I conked out here. Didn't realize I was that tired. Last thing I remember—"

"You were digging through my private photo albums without asking?"

He took a sip. To his relief, he didn't have to choke down a bitter brew to be kind. Was that a hint of cinnamon? "Sorry about that. I was dusting and ran across them."

"Dusting?" She leaned against the edge of the counter and faced him. "The agreement was for you to clean up the trash that you and your buddies made here. I don't think you made the dust."

"Did you just make a joke?" Colt realized someone had put a blanket over him. He studied it for a second.

"I do have a sense of humor when I'm not worried about having some mass murderer or house wrecker in my place." She sipped her own drink, eyeing him over the rim.

"And now?" He stood, folded the blanket, and placed it on the back of the chair before stretching the kinks from his low back.

"Now I think you're still a Neanderthal ex-bull rider with some OCD tendencies."

He chuckled. "Cleaning is my coping mechanism."

"Thanks, by the way."

"For what?" He crossed the room and leaned over the counter.

She played with her earlobe. Apparently he'd discovered *her* coping mechanism. "For not trying to..."

"To what?" He knew what she meant but decided to make her say it.

"You know." She tucked her hair behind her ears and studied her cup like it housed all the answers to world issues, or at least the ones in this room.

"Have you ever thought that men like me might not all be the same?"

She stiffened. "All bull riders are the same."

Relief flooded him. She didn't know his truth. But based on her furrowed brow and stiff shoulders, he guessed she'd encountered a bull rider in her past who broke her heart. And in that moment, he had a desire to mend it. But then he realized he'd been no better than the bull rider she mentioned. How many hearts had he broken?

"Listen. I didn't mean to be so rude," she said in a softer tone.

He choked down his words and decided it best to keep his mouth shut and his attention on the task in front of him. He wanted to stay here for a while, so he needed to keep his mind and thoughts to himself because things never ended well when he was attracted to a woman.

Chapter Six

ALL NIGHT, Saige had tossed and turned and tortured herself with one simple fact. A fact she hoped she'd proven wrong when she had agreed to marry Thomas. How could a good person, a person like her mother, be consumed with thoughts and dreams of a sexy stranger on the night that her fiancé walked out of her life?

Saige eyed the old photo albums Colt had resurrected, the photos full of memories. She abandoned her half-empty mug on the counter and rubbed her temples to ease her mounting headache. The origin was probably the man standing across the counter from her. Maybe her father was right and she didn't need real love in her life, that she wasn't capable of such emotions. The thought put a dark spot on her heart. Like a wound had reopened. She averted her gaze from the photo albums, unable to face her mother's image.

What would she think of her sweet daughter now?

Colt's finger grazed her knuckle. A simple touch with a complicated response. "Hey, you okay?"

"Fine." She downed the last of her coffee and moved away

from him to the other side of the room. "You should call for one of your buddies to come get you. Best to get out of here earlier than later."

She went to her bedroom and searched her nightstand, wanting to find the cowboy Christmas charm her mother had left her, but she couldn't remember where she'd left it. She'd yanked the bracelet from her wrist and tossed it somewhere before fleeing the house with her father.

With a stuttered intake of air, she reenacted that motion. and a flash of memory told her it was in her top drawer. She opened the drawer to find the bracelet with the MH printed on the cowboy hat. The charm that had been passed down for generations lying next to the ghost of relationship past. She retrieved the bracelet with the charm and shoved the door shut, then raced downstairs as if putting distance between her and the memories would keep them far away. She slipped the bracelet on, and it felt right, like it had never been meant to be anywhere but her wrist. This was what she'd come for, to reconnect with her mother and the long history of strong women in her family.

She picked up a throw pillow to punch the dust that had already been beaten out of it by her stranger. Colt had done all the cleaning in the area. She clutched the pillow to her chest and thought for a moment about hiring him to manage the place if he was looking for work, but the more she hugged the pillow to her chest and longed for the warmth of his body, the more she thought better of it.

"Hello? Sorry. I can't hear you. I need a car to get me. Yes, from that group."

Saige dropped the pillow and dared to move closer. Was one of his so-called party buddies too busy to come get him? The man should've realized when they'd left him behind that they were worthless people he couldn't rely on. Like most men in that industry. "What's going on?"

He put a finger to his ear and shouted louder. "Bad connection. I need a car." He moved the receiver from his ear and glanced at it as if to see what the person at the other end was saying then placed it back to his ear. "What's that? Yes. Colt Whitmore."

That name sounded familiar. Maybe they'd crossed paths growing up. She guessed he wasn't a born and bred local based on his choice of boots and the way he spoke.

Wind gusted outside, whistling the announcement of more cold heading their way. No problem. Heater and blankets and fire would be toasty enough. No need for anything else to keep her warm.

"Thank you." He hung up the phone. "They're either going to be here at two or said Tuesday at two. Is the line always that crackly?"

"When it works." She shrugged. "The lines are old. I think my grandfather had them installed when he went off to war. He didn't want my grandmother alone out here. Apparently, it was a party line, and other people would be on when she was. Not sure much has been updated since the 1940s."

"The stories this house must be able to tell, family secrets kept inside these walls..."

His words made her hold the cowboy charm in her hand tight. "Legends, more or less."

"Legend of a charm?" he asked with a tone that made her think he was genuinely interested. "I saw in the photo album that your mother used to wear that charm. She obviously passed it down to you."

"Yes, she did." Saige let it go and eyed the room as if she

could find the answers. "My mother told me to read the story because only her great-great-great-grandmother's words could truly share the tale."

"What did it say?" he asked.

She shrugged. "I don't know." How could she tell him that she'd left the night of her own mother's funeral and never returned to find the book that told the tale of her McKinnie heritage and the legend of the cowboy Christmas charm? Instead of answering, she waltzed to the refrigerator and opened it. "Good thing the cabinet and refrigerator are fully stocked. Guess my cousin did something right. Even if he has let this place go." She sighed and eyed the split kitchen cabinet, the faded wood floors that needed sanding and restraining, and the stain in the corner of the ceiling.

"Sorry to disappoint, but your man had nothing to do with that. The guys I came with stocked the place. Booze and all." He rubbed his head as if still suffering the aftereffects of his hangover.

Great. Her cousin had been collecting wages without working. Time to roll up her sleeves and get her hands dirty. "I'm going to be busy getting this place back into shape. But I can take some time this afternoon to give you a ride into town if your car doesn't show. There's a much more comfortable hotel there for you."

He shrugged. "If that's what you want. Before I leave, I'd like to take a look at the attic for you. Hate to leave without checking for a leak. The ceiling might cave in with the next big snowstorm."

"You don't have to do that." That was the biggest protest she could manage, knowing the truth of his words. She followed him up the stairs to the attic pulldown, where he climbed to the top and then looked down at her. "There a light up here?"

"Burned out, probably. I'll get a flashlight." She raced downstairs and grabbed one of the emergency flashlights and then made her own way up the ladder into the cold, dark space full of junk. A space barely able to fit two bodies, especially a big man like Colt. A man who apparently knew how to fix roofs. A handy skill to have on a ranch.

"Here." She held out the flashlight, barely able to see his shadow.

"Thanks." He flicked it on and shined the light at the far wall. A wall that looked like a crypt with a rotted coffin.

"That doesn't look good."

"Afraid not." He eyed her. "Not sure there's much I can do about that, but you best hire some roofers and quick."

"I don't know when I can get any out here. But I'll call around when I take you back to town." If she left her job behind, her savings would be eaten up quickly if she needed a new roof and other major repairs. What would she do when she was done restoring the place, anyway?

He crawled farther into the darkness and picked at the wood. "Yep, rotted." The light shone on the beam. With the flashlight between his teeth, he pushed on the wood support with both hands and then retrieved the light from his mouth. "Good news, though."

"I could use some of that, especially if it saves me money."

"It will, because the support post is solid."

She crawled up next to him to see and learn about roofing. He had a hint of some cologne that smelled like an invitation to a wild mountaintop on a summer day. A welcomed aroma compared to the musty damp odor of the attic.

The post did appear to be dry. "How do you know about roofs and posts and stuff? Did you grow up around here? On a ranch?"

"No, not around here. But I enjoy restoring old homes. At least I used to."

She sensed he had more to say but he held back. "I was a cowgirl and loved every minute of it while it lasted, but that life doesn't exist anymore. Not really."

The wind whistled loudly through other small holes above their heads. She shifted to get a better look at where the noise had come from, but the board under her cracked. Colt wrapped his arm around her and pulled her against him. "Careful. Need to stay on the planks. That part'll cave in."

She forced one, two, three breaths, unsure if the sudden movement or the fact that he held her tight with his strong arms made her pulse trot at a steady pace. "Thanks. Guess you do know your way around construction."

To her disappointment and relief, he released her, and she settled on her knees by his side. Heat surged to her cheeks, so she was thankful for the muted light. "Guess we should get out of here if there's nothing we can do. I'll add this to my list of things to have fixed. Hope I can find some cheap labor." She climbed down into her past, eyeing the hallway with the wallpaper seam giving way like her armor against this place cracked. It had been easy to ignore her neglect on her mother's family legacy while she didn't stand in the middle of it.

"What's wrong?" Colt pushed the steps back up into the ceiling.

"Funny thing about coming home. You have to face things you hadn't thought about in years. I'm feeling conflicted at the way this place looks. My mother would be so upset to see her home like this."

He chuckled that nervous kind of laugh he did when she had a shotgun pointed at him. "At least you have a home."

"Spend too many years on the road with those buckle bunnies to set down roots, and now you're facing a life without your glorious and famous career?"

"You don't think much of me, do you?" The way Colt's voice dipped with disappointment tugged at her resolve to dislike this man. A man who offered to look at her roof and stayed up all night cleaning her house.

"I don't know you well enough to judge you."

They meandered down the stairs side by side with a back-and-forth glance or two. "Do you think people can change? I'm talking about figuring out who we are, not who everyone else wanted us to be?" he asked.

Her chest tightened. Wasn't that why she was here? To figure out how to be the person that would make her mother proud? "I hope so."

"It's hard in the real world to figure out who you should be because everyone judges you based on who you were before." He stood at the bottom of the stairs and gestured for her to go ahead like a real gentleman.

She grabbed the mop but realized he'd already taken care of the downstairs. "You should try to call again. This time of year, weather turns on you quick."

She headed upstairs to work on one of the other rooms to allow for some alone time to think, away from the delicious downstairs distraction.

With a deep, cleansing breath, she removed her phone from her pocket and collapsed onto the edge of the mattress. She scrolled through her photos. Picture after picture, she eyed herself and Thomas. By the fourth photo, she noticed something. She appeared lifeless, dead inside, and he had a fake smile. Were they ever happy together or just partners in life?

Why hadn't she seen it? Hate didn't begin to describe how she felt about herself. Not when her heart didn't ache to see him again. Her father was right. She was just like him. A woman who'd almost married a man because he was good on paper, not good to her heart.

What kind of woman does that?

A bitter air seeped through the window, causing a chill to shoot up her spine. She'd run out of town so fast, she didn't have anything but her tropical wear for her honeymoon. There had to be some sweaters and warmer shirts around here to wear, so she tossed her phone onto the bed and wrenched open a drawer to find her mother's favorite green sweater.

Colt cleared his throat behind her. She turned to find him leaning into the room with his hands clutching the overhead doorframe in that oh-so-sexy cowboy pose minus the hat. "Line's dead."

Her heart skipped and skittered at the sight of him. If someone looked up in her personal dictionary the perfect specimen to rock her world, they'd find a picture of Colt Whitmore, not Thomas Mauldin. Disgusted and refusing to allow herself to be that naive, stupid, young girl who fell for the bad boy instead of the stable and dependable man she almost married, she shot to the window. A window with a view to the outside world. The view of an incoming storm.

"You know, I was thinking. There's some major work that needs to get done around here, more than one person can handle," he said.

A pinch of worry made her decide to drive him out of town herself. She shoved her phone in her pocket and pushed the drawer to close, but it wouldn't budge. Great, something else to fix. This she could handle on her own, though. She squatted down and tugged it out a little farther and then pushed it in, but something blocked it.

With fingers splayed, she reached deep into the space behind the drawer and felt something. She couldn't reach it, so she jimmied the drawer all the way out and then reached in and pulled out a book.

"What is it?" Colt joined her. "That's old. Look at the gold leaf writing."

"Why would it be hidden back there?" she asked but opened it to discover the words

Francine McKinnie

Her pulse tapped with joy. "It's my great-great-great-great-grandmother's diary. The one who passed down this cowboy Christmas charm."

"Now that's some family history."

She swallowed hard and opened the small, weathered book. "I thought I would never find it. She's one of the seven McKinnie Sisters who took mail-order bride proposals to survive after the Civil War. My grandmother told me those ladies faced such horrors in their youth but lived beautiful and blessed lives later. They were fearless and had huge hearts, were giving and kind."

He sat by her side and placed his hand on her back. "I don't know about you, but I think it would be fascinating to read it."

Her breath caught at his unexpected touch. "I'm sure you have someplace you need to be. I'll give you a ride into town."

"Nope, no place to be."

He'd slept in her barn. She'd found him asleep on her front porch with a hangover. No friends to call to pick him up. Homeless, maybe? Alone? She eyed her great-great-great-great grandmother Francine's journal and realized she wanted to be like the original McKinnie sisters. Brave, giving, charitable, and always ready to do the right thing. "Can I ask you something without offending you?"

The pages in her hand were delicate, so she closed the book gently to face Colt.

"Sure."

"Are you homeless?"

His mouth twitched and he looked at the book in her hands, then the floor, and then back to her. "Yeah, I guess I am. Let's just say I'm out of work at the moment."

"Don't take it as a judgment. Better to be an out-of-work ranch hand than a rich, ruthless businessman or playboy bull-rider Besides, this time of year, there's not much work for ranch hands." With a deep breath, she clutched the book in her hands. Was this her way of redeeming herself, of capturing the McKinnie way by helping a stranger in need? She pushed from the floor. "I'll hire you here for a couple weeks to help with some of the major repairs. You can sleep in the downstairs room, and I'll provide free food. I'll pay you two thousand dollars cash. This'll give you some money to tide you over until something else comes around." She offered her hand, but he hesitated. "It's not charity. It's a job. You'll help me at a discount, and I'll give you a chance to figure out what you want to do next."

He took her hand and shook it gently. "I'd be honored to help restore this place. Maybe we'll both find what we've been looking for."

Her heart bu-bumped, pushing blood to her brain along with ideas. Bad ideas. Ideas that ended with a flash of memory that reminded her of why she'd run from this place before. But he wasn't Trevor, and they weren't involved. Not today, not ever. This wasn't about finding a man. This was about restoring her once beloved home and reconnecting with her past, nicer self. The home where she'd once found joy and love and purpose. And she hoped here, now, she could find that again.

Chapter Seven

AFTER A LONG DAY OF WORK, Colt showered and headed to the kitchen. He wanted to make a nice meal for the woman who thought she gave him a roof over his head. Technically, she had. Technically, he was homeless. Technically, he wasn't lying. Why should he tell her the truth? They didn't even know each other. She wouldn't know who he was until he was long gone.

Not that he felt good about lying, but there would be nothing between them. He wouldn't take Saige to bed. For once in his life, he'd remain platonic and work on himself instead of getting what he wanted from a woman.

He found some sirloin and vegetables that he could whip up really quick into an Asian dish. By the time he heard the shower cut off overhead, he plated the meal and set it at the table. There were two candles there, so he lit them for ambiance but didn't pour any wine. His stomach couldn't handle that yet.

When she entered the room, he pulled out her chair.

She stopped and eyed the food and candles. "What's all this?"

"A thank-you," he said in his most sincere tone. He was thankful because he didn't have to return to the real world yet.

"I'd say you didn't have to, but if we want to eat, you should probably do the cooking."

Was that humor? Her hair was down around her porcelain skin, and the green sweater she wore made her eyes pop, not to mention how it accentuated her curves.

She looked straight into his eyes and waltzed over to the proffered chair then bent over and blew out the candles and turned up the lights. "Food is good, but the lights stay on. This is a job, not a date."

Ouch. He hadn't even realized what he'd done. Maybe he was only a worthless Whitmore whose only talent was womanizing. The law was set, and he had no choice but to obey the rules for now, so he moved his plate across from her and enjoyed his meal in silence with an occasional glance to see her enjoy his cooking. It felt good to make a woman smile sweetly.

Once the last bite had been scooped up, she took a sip of water and set her fork down. "That was delicious. You're really a good chef. If this place functioned as a ranch, I'd hire you to be the cook."

"I'll take that as a compliment." He reached for the dish, but she covered his hand in the most delicious touch.

"I'll clean up since you cooked."

"I work here. You don't. I'm an employee, and this is business," he said in a more bitter tone than he'd intended.

The water faucet sputtered before it gave way to a steady stream, and he dumped the dishes in the soapy water.

"Sorry. Guess I was a little harsh. I don't want this arrangement to be like that, but I just don't need any romantic entanglements right now. I need to focus on this place, not on my next failed relationship."

He washed a plate, and she took it with towel in hand. "I'll dry. We'll work together. It can be business without coldness."

"That's an interesting way to put it." He handed her another dish.

The clink of a plate told him she'd put it away on the shelf behind him. "Something I'm trying out. Business with a little heart. Not sure they go together, but that's what I read in my great-great-great-great-grandmother's book." She took another plate from him. "I think I'm going to refer to her as my great-grandma Francine. It's kind of a mouthful with all those greats."

"I agree." He sponged off the forks and knives then went to work on the water glasses.

"What else have you learned from the book?" he asked.

"Not much. I've been working on clearing out that upstairs closet because I think I found another leak." She sighed. "I'm starting to think this house is turning into a hopeless cause."

"Nothing with this much history is worth giving up on. Tell you what. We're both tired. Up for a cup of tea or coffee? We can sit by the fire and read some of that book if you don't mind sharing."

"Sounds good. But how about some hot cocoa, ranch style?"

"Not sure what that means, but I'm game."

She pulled out a saucepan, and he grimaced. "You sure you know how to use that thing?"

"Hush and go sit down. Consider this your break time."

"Yes, ma'am." He saluted and walked out of the room to stir the fire back to life and to watch the moonlight glisten over the freshly fallen snow. The scenery was like a painting, with its flawless beauty.

"Don't you love the peace this place offers? The quiet calmness?" Saige entered and handed him a mug with *Dare to be a Cowboy* written on the side. He silently answered yes, he'd love that life. A dream at best, because that kind of life didn't really exist.

"Yes, and the way the flakes of snow appear to dance their way down from heaven." She tapped the edge of her cup with perfectly manicured nails. This woman looked comfortable here, but her appearance screamed city girl.

He took a sip. The rich cinnamon brew with a hint of Irish cream gave him a kick and coated his tongue in festive cheer. "I bet this place is amazing at Christmas." The image came to him of family around a tree, singing carols, opening presents. "This must've been a magical place to grow up."

"It was until it wasn't." Her eyes went dark and he didn't like it, so he stayed on topic.

"It's like Charles Dickens' *A Christmas Carol* came to life in this place."

"You don't sound like a typical rough-and-tumble, drunken rancher type." She eyed him like a schoolteacher at a naughty pupil, waiting for him to confess his crime.

"A man like me can't read?"

"Can't? No. Choose to? Not often." She took a sip of her own drink, and to his relief, it appeared to take her back to a memory, one he decided to grab hold of to distract her.

"This is a special drink, isn't it?"

She nodded. "One passed down through generations. It was said that this drink brought my great-grandma Francine's husband, Walt, back to life after a severe storm trapped him in the barn. A whiteout where he couldn't find his way back to the house."

"I love this."

She dropped her cup to chest level. "What?"

He backed up before she ran him out of the house based on that sassy, pursed-lipped look of hers. "The stories of your ancestors. Nothing that interesting in my past. I'd love to know more about this place and the story of that cowboy Christmas charm."

She lit up like the North Star that guided men to their destination in the dead of night. With her drink in one hand, she picked up some throw pillows, tossed them down by the fire, and settled on one of them, so he assumed the other was for him and took his seat by her side, eyeing the fire as he leaned against the side of the couch.

The cozy comfort and companionship lightened his mood to a level he didn't think possible when he'd boarded that plane to escape his father and the media coverage. Never did he ever think he'd find this kind of peace in his life's storm.

She set her cup down at her side, opened the old, worn book with gentle care, and began reading.

"The world I once fell in love with has become disloyal and dangerous. Walt and I are in search of new lives far from the lawlessness and greed. We have sold our home and belongings in Seattle to head east. Strange... When I boarded that ship to sail out here, losing so many during the journey, I never thought I'd gone too far. But now, with children in our laps and one in my belly, we move to a new place. A place of possibilities to grow and cultivate new lands and new life. Walt vows to build a home big enough to have all my sisters and their families come for Christmas this year. My heart swells at the idea of reuniting with

my dear sisters after so many years. However, I must pause. Not because I doubt my husband. He's proven himself capable and a man to conquer any obstacles. It's the unknown of life that frightens me now that we have wee ones to protect. But when politics and threats knock at our door, civilization no longer seems safer than the lands of possibilities."

Saige paused and took a sip, but he couldn't hold his tongue when she flipped a few pages without speaking. "Did they do it? The house, I mean. Did they all get together by Christmas?"

A distant howl punctuated this land's wildness and his respect for anyone willing to take this on in a time before cars and neighbors.

She squinted, moved her face closer to the writing, and flipped pages several times back and forth. "I'm afraid the wrinkled pages are worn and writing smeared as if it's been wet at some point."

"Can I see?"

She passed the book to him, her fingers grazing his for a pulse-strumming moment, but she withdrew and took the adrenaline with her. He eyed the script but only made out words like *worst snowstorm*, *trapped*, and *hopeless*.

"Maybe this is the story you heard about where he was trapped in the barn."

She shrugged and retrieved the book from him as if she didn't trust him with such a precious family heirloom. "It could be." After another sip of her drink, she turned a few more pages.

"I don't think that Christmas turned out the way she'd hoped, though." Saige's voice dipped to sorrow. "A group of men including her husband set out one night after a murderer." She gasped.

"What is it? Was he killed?" He found himself more invested in this story than any business proposal he'd created from scratch, delivered, and sealed the deal.

"No." She crossed her legs and leaned forward, pressing her fingers to the antiqued pages that looked like someone had spilled tea on them. "Here it is. The cowboy Christmas charm." She sucked in a breath and her teeth toyed with her bottom lip in a distracting, alluring way.

"Go on," he nudged her.

She cleared her throat as if to deliver a speech to a large crowd.

"I begged him not to go, with the baby due anytime, the children and me alone. I couldn't face a loss so great, and too many men had fallen to this band of bandits already. I came here to flee the dangers of the city, only to fall into a wild, merciless people in a beautiful, merciless land."

Colt clutched his cup between his hands as if waiting for the pivotal moment in an epic Western film. Would the hero get the girl like in a romance or die trying like a Nicholas Sparks book his stepmother shared with him once when he'd found her crying in her room? He thought his dear old dad had stepped out on her, but it was a book that had brought her to tears. That was the moment he realized his father loved his stepmother more than he'd ever loved Colt's mother. That didn't mean he'd remain faithful to her, though.

A twinge of hatred pinched him, but he swatted it away and refocused on the story in front of him. "What happened?"

"Walt knelt before me in front of the fire and pressed something into my hand. He said that it was a Christmas gift he'd had handcrafted in town but that he wanted to give it to me now. I opened my hand to find a cowboy Christmas charm on a small

string. He took the string, tied it to my wrist, and said, 'Keep this close for it's my promise that I'll return and make our world a brighter, safer place. A place where generations will live and grow and find great happiness. A ring represents a commitment to live our lives together. This represents my promise to always be your cowboy and to always be with you on Christmas.'"

Tears rolled down Saige's cheek. To his surprise, the sight tightened his own throat and misted his eyes. He took her hand in his and held it tight. "You okay?"

"Yes, more than okay. That love they shared. Pure, passionate, promising. Promising of something beyond what I've known in the last decade." Her chin dropped to her chest. "Then, men were real and honorable and women had open hearts. Not like today. Those kinds of relationships are extinct."

Chapter Eight

SHE TURNED THE PAGE, and her heart sank. Unreadable. Not one word legible. "If only my mother was here, I'd know the truth of what happened."

Colt shifted closer to see the book, too close. His arms pressed to hers, his face inches away. She bucked away and slammed the book shut. Her emotions swirled faster than a winter wind. "Nothing else legible. We need sleep. Tomorrow morning, we'll gather a list of supplies and go to town to get what we need. I don't know how long the weather will hold out, and with no service, we won't know until we can check the report when we get there."

He blinked up at her as if to read her innermost thoughts, but her thoughts were as vague and confusing as the swirly letters in the diary she held tight in her hands. "We should go over some ground rules if you'll be working for me."

His brow hitched, but he didn't say anything. He stood and took her mug with him to the kitchen as if his daily duties included washing dishes.

"Is two thousand dollars in two weeks agreeable to you?"

"Too much." He turned on the kitchen water and washed the mugs then dried and put them away. The man was clean, she had to give him that.

"Not when you realize how much I'll be working you. You'll be working ranch hours, sunup to sundown with only meal breaks. Evenings are your own, but I don't plan on cleaning up your drunken mess or dealing with it, so no alcohol unless I say. You'll remain on the ground floor unless personally invited upstairs for work purposes."

His mouth quirked into a sexy grin.

"And the invitation will only be for work purposes," she added with a stern voice.

He crossed his arms over his chest. "I am not a man who would ever need or want to force a woman into any kind of unwanted or uninvited pleasure."

The way his voice dipped deeper on the word pleasure stirred her own fire, but she doused it with the realization that the man who stood before her was like the one she once knew years ago. Before the thought took root, she ripped it from her mind and tossed it far away. No reason to entertain such drama when she was looking for a new life, not reliving bad memories.

"Anything else?" he asked with a lean into the wall like nothing she said sounded unreasonable, but she wanted him to know how much he'd have to work or she wouldn't pay him. "Listen, and I do mean listen. This work will be long and not as thrilling as you're used to. I don't need you to start something you're not going to finish, so if you have any doubts, speak up now. I'll hire a hand in town to come out to help."

"This time of year? I don't think that'll happen." His playful smile flattened, and he moved in like a wolf to attack. She took a step back, and he paused his advance.

"Listen, and I do mean listen. If I give my word, I keep it. Yes, I'm a passionate man, but an honorable one, too. That cowboy charm wasn't a legend, a man like that still exists in this world. Sometimes you just have to open your eyes to see him."

"Stop. None of that."

"What?" he asked in an innocent tone.

She drew circles with her pointer finger in front of his smug expression. "That."

"I'm not sure what you mean..." That grin made a reappearance and bowed.

"I mean, there's not and never will be anything between us. I came here to figure some things out. The last thing I need is a man like you stirring things up around me."

"Stirring things up?" he asked, pressing her for more information.

Information she wasn't about to unpack from her memory trunk. "Are you agreeable to the terms or not?"

"Agreed." He held out his hand.

She thought about not shaking it to avoid his touch, but that would only give him reason to think something that wasn't there. With one firm grip and dip, she yanked her hand away. "Glad we've reached terms."

"Not exactly."

She paused her exit and crossed her arms over her chest. "What do you mean?"

"I mean, I have one more job while I'm here." He ran a hand through his short hair and pressed his palm to the wall above her head, leaning into her, too close.

Her breath caught between shoving him away and pulling him closer.

"I'd like to teach you to cook." He eased away in a casual, smooth move. Boy, he was good.

"I'll stick to what I'm good at, and you can do what you're good at. What else can you do besides fix roofs and cook?" she asked, her breath coming a little quicker than normal.

"Anything. I'm good with my hands."

His words sent tingles down her skin.

"I'll begin work on the attic tomorrow after breakfast, before the next storm arrives. We should hit the sheets."

She snapped her attention to him.

"To sleep." He put his hands on his waist and leaned back, appearing pleased with himself, but then his mouth dropped along with his hands. "You know, not all men are bad. You need to find one worthy of you."

"Really? Who's good enough for me, then? You?"

He let out a short breath. "No one. And I know that no matter how hard I try, I'd never be deserving of your affection."

She faced him. "Or maybe I'm not deserving of you?"

He winked, turned on his heels, went to his room, and shut the door, leaving her heart pounding. No time for wayward thoughts, though, so she took a quick, cold shower and climbed into bed, where she opened the book and tried to make out more words. At some point, her lids grew too heavy and she drifted off to sleep. Sleep full of dreams about a cowboy, a Christmas charm, and a promise of forever.

HE DIDN'T LOOK BACK at her in fear he wouldn't close the door. He collapsed on the bed, exhausted after being up most of the night before. Despite the heaviness of his muscles and the fatigue he felt in his arms and legs, sleep escaped him.

His thoughts drifted to the beauty upstairs. Original in every way, from her shotgun pointing, fire red hair, determined strong personality to her tender touch and soft voice. Most women were one or the other—overly stern and angry all the time or too sensitive and crying all the time. Saige was both and neither. A conundrum he wanted to solve.

Distant howls echoed outside, and he thought about Francine and Walter living here all these years ago. A man brave enough to face this wilderness with a wagon full of babies and a wife. He couldn't even face a real relationship.

He shoved off the covers and paced the floor. Could he make that long walk down the aisle, or was his father right and he'd never commit to a woman? Saige drifted into his mind. A woman he barely knew at the end of the aisle sounded better than any of the ones he'd dated and mated as his stepmother would put it. The mail-order bride thing always sounded so ridiculous, but if Francine and Walt shared love, maybe strangers *could* fall in love. If he had to make a choice now, he'd marry that firecracker upstairs before the fortune seekers in Los Angeles.

The insanity of his thoughts drove him back to bed, where he managed to drift away at some point, only to be haunted by nightmares of reporters and disappointment and judgment, but it turned at some point into something different. When the sunshine flooded in, it woke him from a delicious dream about riding horses through the mountains with Saige.

Smoke seeped through the bottom of the door. A fire alarm blared. He raced from his room to discover Saige in the kitchen waving a towel around. Smoke plumed from the stovetop, where he discovered charcoal he assumed had once been food, although he wasn't sure what kind. He grabbed the oven mitt, dumped the pan into the sink, and poured water over it. Then he removed the battery from the alarm and opened a window an inch.

"I thought we agreed I'd do the cooking," he teased, but when he faced her open-mouth, wide-eyed expression, he took a step back. "What is it? Did you get burned?"

His heart skipped with fear, so he took both her hands and studied her arms but didn't see anything, allowing his pulse to slow.

"I'm fine." She sounded winded. Her gaze drifted from his eyes to his chin to his stomach to his groin to his feet. "Um...I think you're already fit to be a cowboy."

He glanced down and realized he ran out so fast, he was standing there in his boxers. "Isn't that a song?"

A winter chill beat against his bare chest, but when she reached up and brushed her fingertips across his stomach, his body turned hot. Her chest rose and fell with deep, quick breaths.

The aroma of a spring day overpowered the charred odor in the room. He leaned in, swiping his nose up the side of her neck to investigate. Sure enough, it was her.

She moaned, and he thought he'd lose his mind from want, but she stepped back one step, her back pressed to the wall, so he didn't crowd her. To his relief, she continued her exploration of his body to his chest, neck, cheeks. He turned his head and pressed a kiss to her palm, wishing it was her lips.

"I've never met a man who was smart, could cook, with a rancher's body."

"See, a man can be kind, sophisticated, and powerful."

"But no one's perfect." Her fingernails grazed his chin and continued down to his collarbone. "I keep searching, but I don't see the bad boy full of horrific flaws."

"Everyone has flaws." His heart double-timed, and he was sure she'd feel it.

She blinked up at him and asked, "Then what's yours? What will you do to hurt me if given the chance?" She cleared her throat and fled the room. "We should get to work."

Her retreat and belief he was some monster irked him. It was one thing to be labeled the playboy with no family loyalty, but he'd never crossed a line. "I'm the bad boy employee who wants to take advantage of you and then walk away." It wasn't a lie, but it wasn't the truth either. All he wanted was to hold her, kiss her, pull her into bed with him, but then what? Nothing. He wasn't capable of more than a one-night stand, and Saige McKinnie wasn't that type of woman. And something told him she deserved better. Better than him.

Chapter Nine

THE TEMPERATURE inside this morning matched the outside world each time Colt entered the room. "I'll need you to instruct me on how you like your coffee." He placed a large plate full of way too much food and then stood at the kitchen counter to eat his.

He'd remained a few steps from her since he'd dressed. Had she crossed the line admiring his body? What red-blooded woman wouldn't admire a work of art?

He remained straight, shoulders back, arms tight against his thin T-shirt she wished he'd cover with a baggy flannel. He caught her eyeing his broad, impressive chest. "I'll put a shirt on. It was warm in here while I was cooking."

"No." The word shot out of her mouth like a disobedient toddler without a coat in the first fallen snow. "I mean, you can sit at the table to eat."

"I wasn't sure about proper etiquette for a boss and worker on this ranch. I wouldn't want to make you feel threatened." He chugged some orange juice then lifted his plate and sat across from her.

To her dismay, she missed the ease of the charismatic man he was only an hour ago. She retrieved two mugs from the cabinet and went to work on the coffees, figuring to make him a special one as a peace offering. After all, they'd have to work together for the next two weeks. It would be better if they got along. "Listen, I apologize for being direct earlier."

The sound of a fork scraping his plate told her he wasn't going to wait for her to sit down before he ate. So much for his gentlemanly and honorable side.

"Direct is one thing, and establishing boundaries isn't bad either. But for the record, I'd never force myself or take liberties with any woman. I have a baby sister, and if any man ever harmed her..." His voice sounded distant and dangerous.

She finished up the coffees and took them to the table in the dining room, where she found Colt gripping his fork so tight she thought he'd bend it. "I never meant to insinuate that. It's just that I don't know you and you're in my house. Would you want your baby sister to do any less with a stranger?"

He loosened his grip. "I'd want her to deadbolt her room, put a dresser in front of it, and sleep with that shotgun of yours."

She chuckled. "Now I don't feel so bad for a few harsh words."

After a bite and a sip of coffee, after which he rewarded her with a big grin, he placed his cup down, dabbed at his mouth, folded his hands, and looked at her. "What do you want to know?"

She cut a piece of sausage and shrugged. "What do you mean?"

"You said I'm a stranger so you have to protect yourself. I can respect that, so tell me what you want to know."

The heater cut on with a clu-clunk, and she worried it might need to be fixed, too. That list would be two columns on five sheets of paper at this rate. Would two weeks be enough time to Band-Aid this place for a winter?

She popped the piece of sausage into her mouth and savored the rich peppery flavor before she thought about his question. "Your sister. Tell me about her."

His eyes lit up and shone with such love, it chipped away the ice covering her stone-cold heart. "A handful of beauty, grace, and attitude." He scooted around his eggs and sighed. "She has me wrapped around her pinky and tied up in an ornate bow. I'd do anything for her. Anything that I can." His voice dipped to disappointment.

"Your father?"

"Best I stay away. I need to be my own man, not my father's son. I'll never be good enough for him." The way his gaze drifted to his coffee and his fork moved mindlessly around the plate made her want to change the subject. No reason to make him drum up bad memories when she didn't want to herself.

"I'm sure you're a great big brother. Maybe you can call her when we go to town this afternoon."

He smiled, a sweet, innocent kind of joy. "I'd like that."

They ate half their meal before Colt downed some coffee and set his fork down. "Tell me, did you make out any more of the book?"

Images of a cowboy down on one knee in front of her promising to always love her and cherish her churned up her breakfast. "No, none." She needed to move on from personal to work before he twisted her up inside even more. "We should get to work. I'll start making a list of things down here. Can you check out the roof and exterior of the house—oh, and the heater?"

He pointed his fork at her plate. "You didn't finish your meal."

"That's enough to feed four of me." She stood, rubbing her belly. His eyes watched her hand as if he had a thought he wanted to share but didn't.

"What is it?" she asked before she thought better of it.

"I was just thinking about your great-grandmother Francine. Can you imagine being alone here with an unfinished house, children at your feet and one in your belly, and watching your man leave in a time where women had no real rights?"

His observation took her by surprise. A man like him considering women's rights? Of course, if he loved his baby sister that much, he must've thought about such things. "Tell me, how old is your baby sister and what kinds of things do you do with her?"

They both moved their plates to the kitchen, but she took his and shooed him away. "You cook, I clean."

"But I'm the hired help," he reminded her, making her regret her words, but they had to be said or she might not remember her position and cross a line she didn't want to at this time in her life.

"On a ranch, everyone is hired help, even the owners. Just tell me about your sister while you finish your coffee."

He retrieved his coffee from the dining table and returned to the kitchen, leaning against the counter. "Tea parties. That's her favorite."

"Seriously? I can't picture you at a tea party." The hot water scalded her hands, so she jerked away.

He grabbed ice from the freezer and held it to her fingers while checking the redness.

"I'll look at the hot water heater settings while I'm at it, too."

His touch did more to distract her than the ice did soothing the burn. She swallowed so loudly she thought that howling wolf from last night could hear it. "Tea party, huh?" She tried to keep the conversation moving so she wouldn't think about the way his touch made her body wake up from a long hibernation. A ten-year-long sleep. Her skin hadn't tingled or her breath caught like this since...since Trevor.

No, she wouldn't give that jerk a second of her attention. But what if she ran into him in town? Reasonably, he could've moved back here if his rodeo career hadn't continued. Which it probably hadn't this long.

"What is it? Does it sting too badly?" He blew warm breath over her hand, and she thought she'd melt from his attention.

"No, I'm fine." She tried to tug her hand from his grip, but he set the ice aside and checked her skin, running his finger over her knuckles. Her body responded as if he'd hit a happy button no man had ever discovered.

"You'd be surprised what a good female's love can do for a man."

She snatched her hand away. "What?"

He grinned, a dimple-distracting type. "My sister. She changed me from the moment she told me she loved me. That I was her hero."

"Oh, right. Your sister."

He returned to his coffee, allowing her to take in a full breath and hold her hands under cold water before washing the next dish. "We should get started on that list."

With one last gulp, he handed the mug to her and left the room. The sound of the attic steps being taken down squeaked from above, and she knew she had a safe enough distance to relax without having to keep up her guard. At this rate, she'd be exhausted by the end of the day, let alone the end of the week.

She finished the dishes and headed to the dining room to check out the outlet she'd noticed had a burn mark on it. The last thing she wanted to deal with was a fire, but when she spotted the worn photo of herself at seventeen, an inferno erupted inside her.

A photo of her bull-riding jerk of an ex. She tossed the photo to the floor as if it was dangerous. It *was* dangerous.

She held tight to her cowboy charm and realized the truth. It wasn't her fiancé running off that had broken her, because her heart had been crushed years before. And in that moment, she realized why she'd become the backstabbing, heartless businesswoman to make her father proud. Because she had no functioning heart since that day ten years ago. Since the day of her mother's funeral.

Chapter Ten

THE MORNING SUN came and went, and he'd only had time to look at the roof and the water heater. He stopped long enough to make some sandwiches, but to his disappointment, Saige didn't sit to eat, only took a bite and then wrote something down then walked to another area and repeated.

After another few hours of checking the outside, clearing out some of the gutters, and climbing up on the roof outside, the sun dipped below the mountain. It wasn't until light began to fade that he realized there'd be no trip into town today. Not that it mattered. Even if he tried to call his sister, he'd probably never reach beyond some polite servant in the house making an excuse.

He climbed down the ladder and went inside to start dinner, where he found Saige on the floor pulling things out of a box and tossing them into a large trash bag. "Hey."

"Hey." She tied the end of the bag then tried to drag it across the floor.

"Here, I'll get that." He took the bag with little argument

from her and hauled it to the garage with the rest of the stuff she'd purged.

He returned to find her rubbing her neck.

"Why don't you take a break? It's obvious we're not going to make it to town today. I'll get dinner started, and then I'll shower."

"You sure? I've never seen a man work so hard. You deserve a break."

Funny... He'd never been accused of being a hard worker before. The day had flown by, and it hadn't felt like work. He'd liked the hands-on labor instead of sitting at a desk or table for hours and hours.

"I'll rest after dinner." He pulled the stuff from the fridge and began chopping some fresh vegetables. He wrote down a few things on his list, like fresh herbs and heavy cream and some Hoisin sauce to make a great Asian dish. Cooking kept his attention on what was in front of him, which gave him a break from all the regrets he faced in his past.

His attention wavered, though, when he heard the pipes clank and clammer, announcing Saige slipping into a hot shower. He was a gentleman, but that didn't mean his thoughts didn't go to the beautiful naked woman only one floor up from him. He'd never change. He'd always be the playboy with no real commitments in life. What was the point, if all you did was sign a piece of paper then break that promise a year or two later?

Wind picked up outside the window, so he peered out and saw dark clouds crawling over the peaks. He sautéed the vegetables, whipped up a quick sauce, and had thrown some chicken in the oven by the time Saige came down in a form-fitting top and hip-hugging jeans that made him do a double take. Her red hair flowed around her thin shoulders. At that sight, he knew he needed some fresh air and some cold therapy. This behaving like a gentleman was harder than he'd thought it would be. Yep, idle hands led to roaming minds. "Hey, I'm going to cut some more wood. Looks like a storm's coming. Can you stir the sauce while I'm gone?"

"You sure you trust me with that?" She smiled, her bright-white teeth, and sweet berry-colored lips lighting up the darkening room.

"I think I can trust you to stir." He stepped away, giving her space—or giving himself some. He wasn't sure which at this point as he headed out for more firewood. He welcomed the exercise so he'd be worn out enough to sleep, because last night he'd tossed and turned thinking about Saige only a few dozen steps away from his bed. He was a man. He couldn't deny he wanted to rush up there and take her in his arms and enjoy her all night. It's how he behaved that mattered.

By the time he finished chopping wood and hauling it inside, his arms were too tired to worry about lifting Saige and carrying her off to bed. Snow dotted the horizon, and the wind picked up, infiltrating his open coat. The sweat from chopping wood cooled and chilled him.

Snow came down in bucketfuls by the time he carried the last load in and dropped it on the floor. "Sorry about the mess. I'll clean it up." His voice shook more than his body.

"You'll do no such thing." She grabbed his coat and tugged it off then rubbed his arms. "You've done enough for one day. Go get in the hot shower and warm up. I'll get dinner set on the table by the time you finish."

"It's fine. I'll—"

"Do as you're told. I'm the boss, remember?" She winked, a playful smile appeared, and she swatted him on his butt. If she only knew what her words and touch did to him, she wouldn't be so quick to let her guard down. Still, that wasn't an invitation.

"Yes, ma'am. I'll be back." He hopped into the shower and savored the warmth but made quick work, because as much as the hot water soothed his chill, the thought of having dinner with Saige drove him to dress and return to the dining room.

Lights flickered before he could get his shirt on. They stuttered and went out for a few seconds but came back on before he could pull his jeans up to his waist. But then they cut out completely, leaving him in darkness with one sock on. He managed to feel around until he found the other wool sock, pulled it on, and then found the wall that led him to the door that led him to the kitchen, where he spotted the flickering lights of two candles at the dinner table.

"I thought candlelight dinners were against the rules," he teased.

She pulled out a chair and gestured for him to sit down. "No rules when it comes to winter storms. I made that much out from the book while you were in the shower."

He adjusted his collar that felt a little tighter than usual and sat down. "Um, okay. What else did you learn from the diary?"

"Not much. I figured I'd try to read some more tonight, but looks like there won't be a lot of light for that."

Armed with a fork in one hand and a glass of wine in the other, he decided he'd be safe, despite the romantic setting with a beautiful woman in front of him. If only the feelings were more than physical, if only he was capable of committing to one woman, he could be home with his baby sister and behaving in public like the man his father wanted him to be. Apparently, being a scoundrel behind closed doors wasn't a problem. His father had perfected that while married to his mother.

"A firefly for your thoughts?"

"Huh?"

She cut her chicken and took a bite. Her eyes closed, and she moaned. Maybe he could suggest a rule not to moan while sitting alone together by candlelight, yet the joy on her face made him feel good about providing a meal for her she enjoyed.

"It's something my grandmother used to ask me whenever I looked like I was thinking about something." She took a sip of her wine and cut another piece of chicken. "I asked her once what that meant, and she said she never understood why people thought money was so important."

"What did she say?"

"She said that sitting on that front porch on a spring night and seeing the fireflies dancing under the moonlight was worth more than any old penny."

He envisioned the scene and wished he'd have the opportunity to see that someday. "I can agree with that. Especially with inflation."

She laughed, a delicate, sweet sound that he wanted to hear again. The serious woman with the stone attitude he'd met two days ago softened.

He eyed his wineglass but kept his hands busy cutting his chicken.

"I assume you drink, based on the condition I met you in." She poured some wine into his glass.

He took a sip of his wine, enjoying the oak and currant. "Not such a great first impression. I hope I've earned your respect since that incident."

"You've done more than that. I'd say you earned the title of friend."

"Oh, no. I've been friend-zoned." He laughed heartily and held his glass up as if to toast. "The kiss that will never be."

"It could've been a great kiss," Saige mumbled.

"Still could be." He quirked a brow but then directed his attention to his food, not wanting to push too hard when he knew it wouldn't last beyond a moment.

The storm roared to life outside, warning that it could be a long and cold night. The heater didn't clank to life, and he realized despite it being gas, there had to be an electric starter. "Is there a generator somewhere besides the one I found in the basement?"

"No. That was on my list of things to purchase in town. One more thing my cousin didn't buy that I sent him money for." She huffed, and that air of bitterness made an appearance.

He didn't want that attitude to get between them getting to know each other again, so he poured her some more wine. "Why don't you take the book and relax by the fire? I'll make quick work of the dishes and join you. Best we stay close to the heat."

"I'll go gather some blankets and pillows from upstairs." She took a few hearty sips of her wine and smiled. "Nice Cabernet."

"Thanks. I like a good Cab or Merlot."

As she left to gather the bedding, he cleared the dishes, washed, dried, and put them away, and then grabbed the bottle of wine and joined Saige by the fire.

"Good thing you chopped all that wood. Based on the look of that storm, this could last all night, maybe even days."

He didn't mind being snowed in, wrapped up by a fire with

Saige. The idea warmed his insides. He topped off her glass and poured some for himself then snuggled down in front of the fire with her. "Find anything else in the book?"

"Not really. I discovered a section about how a storm blew in and she thought all hope was lost. She clung to the charm, but the last few pages of her entries are unreadable." She sighed and set the book carefully on the side table. "A mystery we may never be able to unravel. If my mom was here, I could ask her more."

"I'm so sorry. You must miss her a lot. You left here after her passing, right?"

She stiffened, and he backpedaled, trying to keep her easy like a new horse edging into training. Not that he knew anything about training horses, but he thought he'd like to learn. "I know that you're hoping to fix this place up. What are your plans for it when you do?"

The fire cast a glow over her snowy-white cheeks. Those emerald eyes glistened in the dim light. "I'd love to turn it back into something functional. A working ranch or bed and breakfast." She shrugged and drank her wine then rested the glass on her knee. "Don't really know yet."

"Dude ranch? I hear people pay a ton of money to go work on a ranch. Never understood why people wanted to pay to work, but it's a thing." His shoulders ached from chopping wood, so he set his glass at his side and rubbed the base of his neck.

"I told you that you work too hard."

How could he tell her it was to curb his desire for the beautiful woman at his side? "Hard work never hurt anyone."

"I'm not so sure about that. Sometimes we use work to avoid things." She lifted her glass. "Here's to less work and more living." The word living came out as *siving*. Apparently, she didn't drink much.

Not that he could judge after the other night.

"You know Thomas? He's my ex-fiancé. Well, Thomas did me a favor obliterating my life by dropping a prenup on me five minutes before we were due at the altar."

He shifted, feeling uncomfortable. For some reason, he didn't like hearing about her with another man. A man she was set to marry. If he could change the subject, he would, but it was obvious she wanted to share. And since she hadn't wanted to share much with him so far, he had to let her talk. "Really? How's that?"

"Forced me to see that I'm a heartless witch who only cares about business. That's all either of us cared about. What kind of marriage would that have been?"

"Maybe he did you a favor. Marriage is only a contract, and if you don't want to sign, then you shouldn't."

Her hair fell over her face, and he couldn't see her expression to read her emotions, so he brushed it back behind her ear. To his shock and delight, she leaned into his touch.

"You sound like him now." The way she moved her cheek against his hand drew him closer. "But you're nothing like that heartless businessman. I never want to be with another man who is my partner. I want passion and romance but with a man who is true and honest. Maybe this place is softening my defenses."

Conviction knocked and whispered that he should consider telling who he was. "Do you think you'll ever forgive Thomas for what he did?"

She downed the last of her wine then picked up his glass and took another sip. "How can I be mad at him when he was right? We were no more than partners. No passion or desire or real love." Another gulp of wine, and then she continued with his glass swaying back and forth in front of her. "Men are either all business and no desire or all desire and no honor."

He coiled into himself. Was he both but neither of those things? Contracts, passion, but dishonorable.

She downed the last of his wine and set the glass on the stone hearth. He moved it to the table in fear it might shatter too close to the heat. The way she'd shatter if he told her the truth. She was sitting next to a businessman who had no honor or ability to commit to anything.

"You know. I'm thinking my stone heart might be cracking thanks to you." She pressed her pointer finger to his chest, and her head rolled to one side, hair falling over her cheek. "Not just my heart. Other parts of me are defrosting."

He swallowed hard. When she leaned into him, he sat on his hands, trying to remember she'd been drinking and he didn't want to do something he knew he'd pay for tomorrow. "It's good to let go of things when they don't work out."

"Shoot. He's the easy one to let go of. I know I'm a horrible person for not caring more, but he was right. I couldn't admit it to myself, but I didn't love him. Not like..." Her voice trailed off.

"Like what?".

"Not what. Who." She tossed her hair back and looked at him with hungry eyes. "I want a man who makes me feel alive. The kind like Francine and Walt had. The kind that takes my breath away and I can barely keep my hands to myself in public and never in private. Someone I can't wait to make it home to at the end of the work day and who I never want to get out of bed and leave." She chuckled. "Fantasy, or young, blind love. Heat and passion don't mix with tenderness and true love. Even if it did, I don't deserve it."

He dared to free one hand and tilted her chin to face him, longing to see those forest-green eyes. "I believe love can be hard to find. I've never found it myself. But I've never gone looking."

She scooted closer, dangerously closer. "Why not? Why don't you want to find love?"

"Spent too much time focusing on things that I thought mattered, but here, in this place, I'm not sure they ever did." He dropped his hand to his side.

"Maybe I don't need loyalty and love. Maybe fire and passion will fill the void if only for a night." She sat up on her knees, tossed off the blanket, and took both his cheeks in her hands with hungry eyes.

His breath caught between lust and want. Want for something more than one night with this woman. She deserved better than that. "No." He forced the one word out, though his voice dripped with need.

She shot up from the fireplace and headed out of the room.

"Wait. Where are you going? It's too cold upstairs."

"It's too cold here." She swiped a tear from her cheek, and he realized she'd misread him.

The thought of him hurting her in any way drove him mad, but if he scooped her up and showed her how much he wanted her, he had no doubt they'd have a passionate night, but then what? He'd had plenty of one-night stands over the years. They always left him empty inside. He wanted more, but he had no clue how to get it. A chance. A real chance at real love.

Chapter Eleven

COLT DIDN'T WANT HER, not even for a night. What bronco-loving free spirit didn't want a woman? It would've felt good to let go of the world if only for a moment.

Footsteps padded against the hardwood floors, and a hand touched her shoulder as a body blocked her path to the stairs. Everything processed slower in her foggy brain and the darkness of the hallway.

"You've got this wrong." He caught her in his arms, making her head spin. "There's nothing more that I want than to taste your lips, touch your skin, feel your body against mine, to hold you all night." His grip tightened. He leaned down eye-to-eye with her, but she couldn't make out his expression in the dim light. "But the night would end, and in the morning, you'd regret it and I'd be sent packing."

His breath came in tight waves of passion, stirring her own need, but she stiffened into a solid woman that wouldn't be hurt again.

"I understand. I'll keep my distance." She shrugged from his arms and about-faced, having to catch hold of the staircase spindles when the room continued moving when she'd stopped. No way she'd make it upstairs. "We'll remain boss and employee, so don't worry about keeping your job."

Saige shuffled into the grand room to face the fire and her humiliation. Her head spun, and she held it for a second, trying to make out her thoughts.

"Listen, that's not what I meant." His sigh echoed in the quiet room. The smell of spring with a hint of mystery wafted into her personal space. The heat of him behind her promised his comforting arms around her. "I don't want to leave here yet. Leave you. There's something here I want to explore more. That's what I don't want to risk."

"I thought I could do it, but I can't. Not like this." Tears pricked at her eyes and visions of something from her past flashed, but she shoved the memories away. She'd come here to connect with her mother, not what happened after the funeral. "Can we go back to sitting by the fire? I'm tired and cold."

To her relief, he pulled her into him and kissed the top of her head. "Then let's get you warmed up." His voice was deep and hoarse, and she could tell he was restrained. Could he really be a strong, sexy, charismatic man who knew how to treat a woman and not just take what he wanted?

He guided her to the floor next to him, settled them down with pillows under their heads, pulled her into his arms, and wrapped several blankets around them. His lips pressed to her temple, and he held her hand, studying each of her fingers before lacing them between hers, kissing each of her knuckles. "You're a woman who deserves to be cherished."

"So, we're not just boss and employee. If so, I'm afraid HR might have a problem with this," she teased, trying to lighten the mood she'd created with her fear of being rejected. Was that why she'd clung to Thomas, because he was solid and she never truly had to open her heart to him? Unlike Trevor, who was the opposite of all things safe.

"Friends," he offered.

"Friends with hand-holding benefits?"

"Friends with possibilities."

She slid into him until they were meshed together and his heat kept her back warm, his arms kept her safe, and his sweet kisses along her jawline kept her wanting more.

The fire faded, but to her relief, he didn't move to tend to it. She fought to keep her eyes open, wanting to savor every moment like this. She hadn't felt this relaxed and happy since... since before her mother died. Since before that day when everything caved in around her.

Sleep summoned her, but the dreams haunted her. Visions of a cabin in the woods. She walked up the hill, touched the door. Noises inside told her to run. Run far and never look back. She jolted upright, with fits of tight breaths.

Strong, warm hands cupped the back of her neck and gently massaged. "It's okay. I'm here. It was only a dream."

But it wasn't. It was a memory. A memory she hoped never to face. A memory that she only now realized had been buried for a decade, but being here had stirred it back to life. Only, she didn't want it. She wanted that door to stay closed forever.

Snow continued to fall but had slowed to a drizzle. The white world outside beckoned her to see the life beyond this moment, but she didn't want to look. She only wanted to look at the man by her side promising an escape from the harsh realities of the world.

"Electricity came back on about an hour ago. How about I

fix us some breakfast and you make some of that delicious coffee of yours?"

He offered his hand and helped her to stand, but her head throbbed. "How much did I drink?"

"Enough but not too much. Close to a bottle. I had half a glass."

"Guess I've lost my tolerance since college."

He pulled her in, her cheek pressed to his chest.

Pa-pump. Pa-pump. Pa-pump soothed her even more.

"If you tell me how, I'll make the coffee and you can rest here."

She knew she'd never let him go if she didn't get away quick, and she needed to let go. He'd only be here a couple weeks. What had she been thinking? She hadn't. The wine had been thinking for her. She shoved from him and laughed it off. "No way. My grandmother always said a cowgirl can play, but she better be willing to pay because there's no rest on a ranch."

"Good to know." He sauntered ahead of her and reached the kitchen. "Eggs and bacon okay? I'd love to make something fancier, but I'd like to take a look at another leak I found."

"Sounds great. Might mop up some alcohol in my belly." She grabbed the coffee and the grinder.

"Think we'll be able to go to town today?"

"If the trucks run and there's no sign of another storm. You don't want to get trapped in the hills and mountains in a good snow. You'll never make it out."

They enjoyed breakfast, and by the time she was done eating and working upstairs gutting the guest room, her stomach felt better and her headache was gone.

She made her way out to the front porch, but there were no groaning engines or squeals of the salt trucks in the distance.

Besides, she needed to shovel her car out of the snow since the garage had been too packed full of junk to pull her car into when she'd arrived.

"What's the latest?" Colt exited the house wiping his oil-stained hands on a rag. He looked confident, settled, like he'd been born here on the ranch. She wanted to feel that—settled, happy, open.

"Not going to make it out today." The snow went on as far as she could see, the land like a scene from a Disney movie. Picture perfect and undisturbed.

"I'm afraid I won't be able to get that generator working. It's a goner. I did my best, but I pronounced it dead at 3:32 p.m."

The way he leaned against the doorframe in that *I'm chill and sexy* way made her want to snuggle up to him even more than the bitter chill piercing the holes in her sweater.

"Come on," he said. "You're shivering. Let's go warm you up by the fire while I check out what we have left to make for dinner."

"Good thing you had the place stocked. The few groceries I brought wouldn't have fed two people for a week, and that might be how long we're snowed in."

"Things could be worse. I'll make you a deal. My two weeks doesn't start until we can head to town and purchase supplies."

He opened the door but didn't touch her until he'd gone into the kitchen, scrubbed his hands cleaned, and then joined her by the fire.

That would mean he'd be here longer. Not something she was opposed to at the moment. "I think that's fair. At least you can go sleep in your comfortable bed tonight with the electricity working now," he offered, as if good news, but it wasn't. She wanted to stay right here by the fire in his arms all night.

"Don't count on it. The electricity out here is as reliable as the phone. Could cut off at any moment." She said it as if a possibility, but she'd already decided even if she had to flick that breaker, she'd make sure they had to remain together.

And she did, for five more glorious nights. After all, they were friends with possibilities.

Chapter Twelve

FIVE DAYS LATER, the sun peered out between the clouds, but Colt wasn't sure he wanted to be greeted with such light. Sunlight meant the end of their forced proximity. Their nightly snuggle by the fire.

He didn't dare move, in fear she'd wake. Her long lashes fluttered against her pale cheeks, and he wondered what she was dreaming about.

Could she be dreaming about him? He'd dated girls for publicity and had flings with beautiful women. His stepmother once told him that there was someone for everyone out there, and he'd wanted to ask why she'd married his father, then, but he didn't.

To his disappointment, the roar of a distant engine woke her. She opened her eyes to reveal beautiful, rich, and vibrant green. "Good morning," she whispered, covering her mouth as if scared she had morning breath. He wouldn't care, if he could kiss her. And boy did he want to kiss her. It had been almost a week, a long and torturous time, but he'd done it. He hadn't crossed a line. Could he be better than his father, or did the genes run so deep he'd never be capable of a real relationship with one person? At this moment, he wasn't thinking of another woman—only Saige. How long would that last, though?

"Guess we better get moving if we're going to get into town. Not that I mind our arrangement." She winked but fled from his arms.

They followed in step, him at the stove and her at the coffeemaker, working together to start their day like an old married couple. He liked how it felt to have a partner by his side for daily chores.

He'd never had that. In fact, he'd barely had daily chores. They had servants for that back home, and he worked too much to care about doing anything for himself. Except when he'd snuck down to the kitchen at night to cook some food when he couldn't sleep.

He'd liked that she thought of him as a hardworking cowboy, even if she did seem to have issues with the rough and rugged type. Then again, she had even more issues with the heartless business type. Which was he? Was there another type?

They sat and ate, toying their fingers together after each bite. Maybe he would tell her the truth. When they got into town and they had dinner, he'd slip it into conversation and tell her how he'd left behind the reputation of being a billionaire playboy. Wait. That would be worse. It would be both rough and rugged *and* heartless rich boy. That wouldn't go over well.

He should tell her now, but when he put his coffee mug on the table, she leaned in and pressed her lips to his. It was a chaste kiss, quick and simple, but erupted complex emotions inside him. "For luck. We'll need it to dig that car out."

She smiled and took their dishes to wash. He went to his

cold bedroom, thankful he hadn't had to sleep in there, despite the electricity coming on and then off again. He'd suspected she'd flipped the breaker, and he guessed she suspected he never checked it.

When he returned, dressed for outdoor work, she handed him a shovel then walked into the garage. A few minutes later, an engine chugged, turned over, and then she came out riding a tractor. She managed the machine like a pro.

What a sight, with her red hair flowing behind her against the white snow in the background. Mesmerized, he couldn't remember what he was doing for a moment until she whistled and pointed to the car.

He went to work, and after about an hour, they managed to dig out the car and make a path to the road. That poor little car didn't look tough enough to make it to town, but he wasn't going to point that out right now.

They made quick work of lunch and grabbed their lists to set out for town.

He hesitated at the front porch steps. "You sure about this?"

"About what?" she asked. "Leaving our little hideaway to be around other people?"

She didn't give him time to answer before she teased, "Not really, *friend with possibilities*."

"I like this you. Fun, happy." He dared to plant a quick kiss on her lips but still pulled away before it turned into anything. He eyed the big red barn and imagined horses neighing and cows mooing in the field. He wanted to ride off into the sunset with Saige by his side. "I can see this place as a dude ranch. Kids running and playing with horseback riding, outdoor games, chuck wagons, and hayrides."

"I like your vision." She sighed and eyed the barn herself. "We used to have a dozen or so horses on this property. Riding was a daily activity."

"Sounds amazing." They'd spent a week together getting to know each other, and the person he found beneath the tough exterior softened his heart. Something he wasn't sure how to handle. But he knew a woman like Saige would never forgive him if they took things too far and then she found out about his true identity. That was probably the only reason he'd managed to keep his hands and lips and other parts to himself this long.

He opened the car door and tucked her safely into the driver's side and then joined her for the ride. A ride that took on a new experience when they reached the mountain road. He gripped the door handle so tight he thought he'd break the door.

"Don't worry. We're fine."

"There's two feet and then a skinny rail and a huge drop-off."

"Snow blocks most of it."

"Snow isn't solid," he teased but still wanted out of the car desperately. "Sorry. Not a fan of heights or crashing down the side of the mountain."

"I'll hold your hand if it'll make you feel better."

"Don't take this the wrong way, but no thanks. Keep both hands on that wheel."

She laughed and continued up and around. The road curved and curved and curved.

He'd opened his mouth twice, ready to start a conversation to lead into their dinner convo about his past and who he wanted to be, but each time he tried, either an animal made an appearance or the car slid or the mountain taunted him with its rigid ravines.

A sign appeared ahead. *Welcome to Rock Ridge.*

"You can relax now. It's a straight shot from here."

He let out a big breath of air and unfurled his fingers. "No offense, but it's tough being the passenger. I prefer to be in the driver's seat. I'm not used to giving someone else control over my life."

"Do tell..." She turned and headed down a main road that had houses dotting either side about every few hundred feet.

"I'm a man. The end."

"I'm hoping that's not the end of your story. If so, I'm thinking we're friends with no possibilities."

"Okay, maybe not, but I do like to be in control."

"Do you like to control everything or just cleaning and driving?"

He wasn't sure how to answer that. If he said he liked to control life, he'd be a control freak. If he said he didn't care, then she'd know he was lying.

"Don't overthink it. I'm not judging. Just trying to get to know my friend better. What would your sister say about you?"

A lightness flittered up inside him. "She'd give me that sassy hand on her hip, toss her ponytail behind her shoulders, and say that I needed to get over myself and play dolls with her because it's okay for boys to play with dolls now."

She giggled. "I think I'd like your baby sister."

"You should. She's got an attitude just like yours." He reached over and took her hand, unable to keep distance between them a moment longer.

They pulled into a parking place in front of a large warehouse-looking building with *hardware and feed* written on the side.

"We'll start here. The main section of town is just up there. We'll do a late lunch/early dinner and then head back so we're not driving at night. I wouldn't want to make a wrong turn and end up driving off a cliff."

"Not funny," he grunted.

They'd barely made it two steps from the car before they were holding hands. Everything came natural and easy with her.

Only a few older people milled about in the store, but they were friendly and helpful, and to his shock, no one had a cell phone out. He'd forgotten about cell reception. "Hey, do you mind if I go call my sister? I promise I'll be right back. I'm hoping to catch her between her dance lessons and playtime."

"Of course. No hurry. I'll get some stuff together." She gave him a sideways hug and looked up at him. "But don't be gone too long."

"Because you'll miss me?" He leaned down to steal one more quick kiss.

"No, because I need a big, strong man to help me get the stuff to the car."

"Cold."

"Not as cold as a night sleeping in the barn would be."

"Oh, so that's how it's going to be?"

She sauntered off, and he swore she swayed her hips with extra swish. It worked because he wanted to follow her, not go outside to make a call.

Once outside, he regretted his decision. Despite not having any fresh snow falling, the temperature was still somewhere between bitter and frosty. He dialed the house and willed a nice servant to answer, maybe a new hire who didn't know he'd been banned from their house.

"Whitmore residence."

"This is Colt Whitmore. Please have my sister come to the phone."

"I'm sorry, sir, but she's not here. They're at the hospital."

"Hospital?" Heat surged to his face, and his heart fell like an avalanche to his stomach. "What happened? Is she okay?"

"She's fine, sir. Just needs a couple of stitches. She fell and cut her chin."

"What hospital? Where is she at? I'll call there."

"No need, sir. I'll let her know you called when she returns. Good day."

The phone clicked off, and his anger surged through him. He threw his phone at a bush and let out a long grunt of frustration.

"What's wrong?" Saige was at his side moments later.

His muscles screamed to hit something. He needed to know, now. Part of him wanted to run to the nearest exit and race to California to find out what happened to the only person in his life who ever made sense to him. "My sister. She's been sent to the hospital."

Saige wrapped her arms around him, soothing the beast inside him that wanted to fight the world. "I'm here. Tell me what I can do."

Those words were foreign to him. No one had ever asked him what they could do for him. He'd only ever done for others in his family. "I...I don't know."

She hugged him tighter and then slipped away, leaving an emptiness inside him. She retrieved his phone, dusted it off, and handed it to him. "You call until you find out what's going on.

If you call enough, someone will answer. Trust me, I've done it enough in business. If they don't answer, then leave a message that you know will get them to return your call."

That would work. Threatening to return to embarrass the family further would get a return call. "You're not only beautiful, determined, and sexy, but a genius." He allowed his hand to drift down her shoulder, along her side, and stop at the curve of her hip.

"Guess my manipulative business tactics can be used for good."

"You're a good person, Saige McKinnie. I wish you could see it as I do."

A blush dusted her cheek, and her body softened as if surrendering to his words. Maybe she finally believed him.

"I like how you see me."

He wanted to say he'd like to see more of her, but now wasn't the time. Now, he needed to find out about his sister, so he dialed the one person who would never return his call, his father. But he couldn't leave the message he wanted to in front of Saige. Not until he had a chance to tell her about his reputation. He only hoped he'd proven himself a better man than one who would use and toss women aside. "It's cold out here. Please, go inside. I only want to worry about *one* of the important people in my life."

Her eyes sparkled at his words. "You just need me to survive long enough to pay you."

"How'd you figure me out?"

"You're not so hard to get to know after all."

"When I get off this call, I want to tell you everything about me." He kissed the sensitive spot under her ear. "And I hope you'll open your heart and trust me with it."

She shied away, but he'd make her see he wasn't the man who cared more about a document than sweeping her off her feet. It would be hard to face the truth, but it was about time in his life he started doing that, because living a lie didn't work.

He called his father and waited, but it only took one ring before he was sent to voicemail. "Father, I've been informed that Abbey's injured. You have two choices. Call and let me know how she is and I'll remain the hidden embarrassment of your life, or don't call me back in the next ten minutes and I'll be on a plane home, and I will make sure the media knows of my return." He hung up and paced the sidewalk outside the store.

A man across the street stood there eyeing him as if the small-town resident didn't like the stranger. Colt waved, but the man only about-faced and walked up the road, disappearing into a building marked Barring Construction.

He didn't have time to care because his phone rang. The picture of his stepmother with Abbey appeared. He answered. "I should've known he wouldn't call me himself."

"I know you're upset about Abbey." His stepmother's voice, the woman he'd been accommodating to but never accepting of, sounded tired and upset. For the first time since she'd entered their lives, he had a twinge of sympathy for her. "I want to let you know she's fine. Only three stitches."

His entire body gave way and he collapsed onto the curb, holding his head in his hands. His boots were ankle-deep in snow. "Thank you." One, two, three breaths before he managed to find his next words. "What happened?"

"Honestly? I'm not supposed to tell you, but I'm going to anyway." She cleared her throat. "Your baby sister hasn't recovered since you left. She's been acting out, and this time she fell out a second-story window. She's lucky the tree broke her fall."

"I didn't leave. I was sent away."

"You and I both know your father wanted you out of the media spotlight. You could've stayed in the house for a month or two, but you took off with some Billionaire Bad Boys Club to get back at him. To show the world you weren't his perfect son. If you two would only have a conversation, you'd stop hurting each other. I'm tired of being in the middle. I know I'm the wicked stepmother so you probably won't believe this, but I love you like my own son."

"I'm only ten years younger than you."

She let out a long breath, and he felt a twinge of guilt. "Listen, I know you'll never accept me as your stepmother since you believe I drove your mother away, but you don't know the entire story. He wants you to settle down and take up your torch, but he doesn't want to do to you what his father did to him. He's not upset with you but with himself. For marrying a woman he never loved to please his father."

"What?" The world spun.

"As I said, I'm tired of living with lies and half truths. Your father may never forgive me, but if I ever hope to fix our family, someone has to tell you the truth. Your father never loved your mother, but he didn't want you to know because he never wanted you to think he didn't love you. You and your brother were the prize from those fifteen years of marriage. He fought for custody so you two could have a good life, but somewhere along the way, he got lost in the world of business and didn't realize he'd become his own father until you were gone. He wasn't a womanizing monster who cheats on women. He was an unloved husband looking for love. He found that in me, and he's been faithful. I know you act out because you think you're no better, but you are. You're capable of so much more. That's what frustrates us."

Colt rubbed his temple, trying to reconcile her words with his past. What he thought was his truth. "I don't understand. If all this is true, why didn't he tell me himself? Why hasn't he called me? Why did he forbid me to see Abbey?"

"Because he wanted you far away from this life so you could figure out who you were. He knew you'd never be able to figure it out living this life. You saw it as a curse, but he meant it as a gift."

Words. He heard them, but he couldn't process them. None of it made sense. "I... Just tell me what I can do for Abbey."

A speaker called out in the background, revealing she was still in the hospital. "I have to go. Abbey's fine. Figure out your life, and then come home to us, but don't come back until you're ready to hear the truth and live your life the way *you* want. I'll work on your father while you're gone. He's got a lot of his own baggage to unpack."

"Alyssa?"

"Yes?"

"Thank you. And please give Abbey a hug for me and tell her I love her."

"I will."

The phone clicked off, and he raised his head to look at the world around him, so different than where he'd lived all those years. Could all of what Alyssa said be true? Could he not come from a long line of jerks who used women and tossed them aside when they got bored?

That man he'd seen earlier peered out the front window of the building, but when they locked gazes, he retreated. Strange.

Shaking off his thoughts, Colt knew he needed to return to Saige. He found her at the register, but he couldn't hold back another second. He wanted the comfort, her light to chase away his darkness, so he kissed her, daring to hold it a second longer. The minute he got the chance to tell her the truth, beg her forgiveness, he would kiss her the way she deserved. A kiss she'd never forget.

Chapter Thirteen

SAIGE COULD FEEL the pain and confusion from Colt and longed to help him like he'd helped her find peace in her world in the last couple days. They finished shopping and settled into a booth at the Rock Ridge Diner for a meal. She reached across the table and took his hand. "Here. I got you something."

She pushed across the table a bag that he hadn't even noticed after loading into the car the last of the supplies they'd picked up. "What can I do?"

"A gift for me?" He smiled, lopsided and a little wilted, but he did look a little perkier. He pulled the box from the bag and smiled. "Real snow boots! Thanks." He made quick work of getting off those ridiculous cowboy boots and putting on his snow ones. "I appreciate that. You're a kind soul, Saige McKinnie."

His words made her sit a little taller, but his eyes drifted to the crack in the wood tabletop.

"What can I do?" she offered.

"Nothing. It's fine. My stepmother told me Abbey only got

a couple of stitches." His brave face and forced smile did nothing to convince her.

"I thought we were friends with possibilities. Maybe one of those possibilities is being a good listener and not judging each other."

His face scrunched, lines by his eyes forming, and she knew he was contemplating her words.

The waitress came over and set some menus on the table. "What can I get you to drink? Hey, wait, you look familiar. Here I was thinking you were strangers. Saige, isn't it? We were in grade school together."

A twinge of warning made her retreat to her own side of the table and study the menu, keeping her head down. "Right. Um, I'll have some water please."

The girl with the Mindy nametag tapped her pen against her old-fashioned pad of paper. "Where have you been? You disappeared. Rumor had it your father kidnapped you after your mother passed."

Saige smoothed her napkin in her lap.

Colt slid a menu to his side of the table. "I'll take a water, too. We'll be ready to order in a minute."

Despite his words that were obviously to tell the girl it was time for her to leave, she didn't pay any attention. "Oh, sorry. You still sad over that? You and your mother were awful close—well, almost as close as you and—"

"I'll have the Cobb salad, and if you don't mind, we're kind of in a hurry. We need to get back on the road before the weather changes. Snow has already started falling out there." Saige handed the woman the menu.

"I'll have the same," Colt said.

She wanted to reach over and hug him for making it quick.

Mindy stuck the menus under her arm. "Okay, but you're not getting out of here until you tell me where you've been and why you're back. You know I've gotta know all the gossip to share in town."

She bounced away from the table as if the news of Saige's return would be broadcast to the town in minutes.

"You okay?" Colt asked.

No. She wasn't going there. Not now, not ever. "Past is in the past. No reason to bring it up now. Besides, we're discussing you and your phone call with your stepmother."

"Right." He folded his hands in front of him. "The conversation illuminated things I hadn't anticipated."

She listened, knowing he chose formal words and spoke in a business tone to separate himself from his feelings. Something she'd done herself on occasion. "What did you learn?"

"That my stepmother might not have been the cause of my parents' divorce and that my father may not hate me as much as I'd thought." He ran his hand through his hair. In only a week, it had grown out some, and she liked it wild and untamed.

"But she said something to make you think otherwise."

He nodded.

Mindy returned with their drinks, but apparently, even she saw they were in deep conversation and withered away from their table without a word.

"Go on," Saige nudged.

"I left because I thought my father cared more about his world than about me. I embarrassed him, and he banished me. My stepmother says that wasn't true. That he wanted more for me than what he had."

"What do you think?" She snagged one of his fingers, tugged his hands apart, and held them tight.

"I think I need to tell you something." He gulped and his hands tightened, holding her as if he feared she'd slip away.

"Go ahead. I'm listening."

Mindy returned with both Cobb salads, forcing them apart. Saige leaned back to allow room.

Mindy plopped the check down. "I still can't believe you're sitting at my booth today. My horoscope said something exciting would happen, but I didn't believe it because nothing exciting ever happens in Rocky Ridge." She bent over with hand to her mouth as if to whisper a secret. "Should've known better than to doubt the heavens."

Saige averted her gaze and looked out the window while she mindlessly picked up her fork and stirred her greens. Suddenly, she caught sight of someone outside the window.

Before her brain could register the sight, her pulse hammered in warning. It couldn't be. Not Trevor. Not the boy who'd deceived her all those years ago.

She closed her eyes, and when she opened them, he was gone. Did she imagine it? Snow came down harder, and she knew there was no way she'd spend another minute in town in fear of having her past beat down her future possibilities. "Change of plans. We need these to go. Now."

Colt glanced over his shoulder. "Is it safe to drive back?"

"Yes, if we hurry." Saige looked at Mindy. "Big tip if you grab some boxes fast."

By the time Saige slapped enough cash to cover the bill and tip, Mindy had returned with the boxes. With two swipes, she pushed her lunch into the container and headed for the door. Snow covered the hood and roof of the car.

A quick press of a button started the car, and she headed

out of town. To her dismay, there was no sign of salt trucks, but she wouldn't stay in town a second longer.

"My turn to ask if everything's okay," Colt said.

No way she'd allow that man to take one second of her thoughts. A boy from her past didn't deserve that kind of attention. "We were talking about you. Your father and why you left."

He tapped the side window with his finger but didn't say anything for a minute. "Now's not the time. I can tell you're upset. Talk to me. You just helped me. Let me help you."

He couldn't help. Her father hadn't helped when he ripped her away from her childhood home. Business didn't help when she'd buried herself in it for years. And returning here didn't help because no matter how hard she'd tried all these years to fix what had broken the afternoon of her mother's funeral, it didn't work. None of the pieces had ever fit back together again.

Chapter Fourteen

COLT HADN'T BEEN ready to leave the diner. He hadn't told her the truth yet, but now was obviously not the time. Something had spooked her like a nervous horse. "I'm here to listen. What happened back at the diner? Did Mindy say something?"

Saige didn't respond. She only kept her eyes on the road and leaned forward as if to see through the falling snow.

"You sure you don't want to wait until morning to head back? You said there's a hotel in town, right?"

She pointed through the front windshield. "No time. These storms blow over the mountains so quickly. I checked the weather forecast, and this storm's going to be a hefty one and will close the roads for a couple days. Worse, prediction says icy mix. That'll make it more difficult to pass the roads closer to home."

"Is it such a big deal to stay here, then? The wood delivery won't arrive for a few days, so major roof repairs will have to wait anyway. I promise I'll stay longer." He hoped she'd let him stay longer.

"Best we get back and start on the other work." Her words

were tight and short and fast, but he had to admit the idea of being trapped in the warm house with her again didn't sound torturous in any way.

No phones, no news, stuck in a house with a beautiful and feisty woman with a mind of her own sounded like heaven to him. Maybe when they reached the safety of the ranch, she'd open up and talk to him, and he'd be able to tell her everything.

The tires spun in protest when she turned onto the main road heading toward the mountain pass, but she maneuvered like a well-seasoned northwestern driver.

Silence punctuated the awkward tension in the car, so he touched the radio button and found some music. Pentatonix Christmas songs seemed appropriate. "Mind?"

She shook her head, eyes straight, hands at ten and two, telling him she doubted this decision, too.

"People looked at me strangely in town. Probably figured out I'm some drifter. Glad you don't think I'm a serial killer or anything like that now."

"Not true." A hint of a smile curved the right side of her lips, giving him hope he'd distracted her for a moment from whatever troubled her back there. "Serial cleaner, maybe."

"Deal breaker, huh?"

"More like a deal sealer." She chuckled. "Usually cowboy types drip muddy manure through the house and leave smelly socks on the floor of the bedroom."

"Sounds like you speak from experience."

"I grew up here." She shrugged, but the way her hands tightened on the steering wheel despite the clear path ahead told him there was more to this story.

He traced a drop of melting snow meandering down the window. "I can safely say I'm not your typical rancher." That was honest, if not a little misleading. "And you're not like most girls I've met."

"You mean the kind who throw themselves at you and their entire life is about you and only you?"

He dropped his hands to his lap and studied her for a moment. Her high cheekbones, large eyes with dark lashes, red hair highlighting her silky, cloud-white skin. All of it pieced together into a perfect Renaissance portrait. One that he could stare at for hours and only unlock a portion of her thoughts.

The tension radiating from her screamed that she was pulling away. He didn't like it. "You're difficult to read. Most girls are obvious."

A slick spot in the road took the car to the edge, but she recovered well.

"I've got this. Don't break my dash." She reset her posture and eyes to focus completely on the road ahead.

He let go and relaxed back, trusting his life to Saige. Not a notion familiar to him, but something told him she could handle any challenge in life. Except whatever she faced that drove her to flee town.

The car whined up the small hill at a slow, sluggish pace. Snow came down in a heavy, icy mix, covering the road, but she kept going until it flattened out and they rounded the side of a mountain. There was a break in the snowbank, and he saw why. The snow had slid down, leaving a three-foot barrier from the road to the valley far below. He cleared his throat, about to demand they return to town, but when they reached another turn where tall pines provided a buffer to their slippery death, he decided to keep his fear to himself.

The mountain wasn't done with them yet, though. The hill ahead could be too much for any skill level in this vehicle. But he wasn't sure he wanted to turn back and face that downhill death trap.

The song changed to a happy "Frosty the Snowman" tune, but he thought it should be something more like *The Shining* theme song, with the darkening sky and isolated tree-lined road.

The slush covered the road, and if the plow hadn't cleared recently, they wouldn't be able to tell where the road even existed. He remembered the uphill from the main road where the drop-off was only a few feet away and knew they'd never make that downhill turn safely. "We need to turn back."

"No," she said flatly.

"Don't be stubborn."

"Don't tell me what to do. You don't rule over me," she shot back.

"I don't know what happened back there, but risking our lives isn't the answer. There's a difference between ruling over someone and offering advice."

"Unsolicited." The look she snapped at him told him to retreat, but no way he'd back down from this. He wasn't a bully, but he wouldn't stand by and let someone die because of an emotional issue.

"We've only made it two or three miles, and the weather's already turning."

She raised her hand in the air, and the cowboy charm wiggled in warning. "All you cowboys are the same. You believe women can't think for themselves or make good decisions. I don't need a man to be my hero for a moment."

"For a moment?" He eyed the road ahead. Snow blocked by the trees increased visibility. He needed to calm her, so he reached out and touched her arm. "I don't know what happened to you in that town, but—"

Apparently, he'd lit her fuse because she snatched her arm away. "Don't touch the driver."

They reached a clearing between heavy woods where snow came down in sheets, blanketing the road from view. The right front tire hit something hidden beneath the snowy terrain. A branch shot up and smashed the windshield.

Crack!

The car fishtailed. He shot an arm in front of her on instinct. She jerked the wheel, sending them into a full spin.

The car slid, jolting and bucking like a wild animal over stumps and debris down an embankment.

Screams. His and hers echoed in the car. Trees shot past his view, but they slowed and slowed and slowed until they drifted to a stop, stuck in a pile of snow taller than the windshield. He heaved in a few deep breaths and let out a chuckle.

"What's so funny?"

He lowered his arm and checked to see if Saige had any blood or breaks, but she looked unscathed. "That was anti-climactic."

She gripped the steering wheel with unshed tears glistening in her eyes. Unmoving, unblinking, she whispered, "I can't."

"Can't what?"

She didn't answer, only rested her forehead on the steering wheel.

Drawn to chase her pain away, he unbuckled and rubbed small, soothing circles on her back. "If this is about your ex, I'm sorry he broke your heart, but I'm not him. I wouldn't tell a woman I loved her and then walk out."

She lifted her head as if to study the ice covering the windshield. "You're telling me you've never told a woman you loved her and then broken things off?"

He shifted in his seat, retreating from the warmth of her body, and the elusive connection that sparked between them then vanished. He longed to see her beautiful eyes, so he brushed the hair from her face and dared to look through a peephole to see his hidden truth. A man incapable of loving anyone but himself. Maybe his father was right to send him away.

But he wanted to experience that kind of relationship. The heart-pounding, blood-pumping, can't live without the other person kind of love. If it even existed. Even if it did, he wasn't capable of sticking around long enough to grow that kind of bond. "I've never told a woman I loved her."

SAIGE SWALLOWED HARD, having a moment of believing this man could truly be different. Not a friend with possibilities, but something more. Much more. A man who'd never told a woman he loved her didn't sound plausible, though. "Men usually throw that word around like candy at Halloween."

His knuckles brushed her cheek, sending heat down her neck. The music drifted from the speakers.

Baby, I hope Santa brings you to me.

'Cause it's all I wished for this Christmas Eve.

She eyed the radio, trying to decipher the words as if it were some poem from a literature class written in old English. To avoid looking at Colt and falling for the bad boy cliché she'd left behind that now haunted her, she scanned the windows, looking for an opening to see the terrain.

He had to be a bad boy because a man with the swagger and strength of a cowboy and the sensitivity and sweet tone of a good guy was an oxymoron. A dream. A Christmas wish that, no matter how many years she waited, would never arrive under her tree.

She hadn't realized it until she saw the man who broke her heart standing outside the diner window looking in at her. A face she'd excommunicated from her life and thoughts since the day he'd betrayed her and left her shattered. She'd sworn she'd never give any man the power to do that to her again.

"Guess I did it this time." She groaned. "No way this car is getting out of this embankment. We better get walking before the weather gets worse. Mostly downhill home and a shorter distance."

"Temperature's dropping quick. Are we better staying put?" he asked, worry lacing his tone.

"No. There's no one looking for us." She grabbed the door handle, feeling convicted. Not that apologies came any easier for her than her father, but change was what this trip was all about. "I'm sorry for getting us into this. You're right. Sometimes my Irish temper gets in my way."

"Doesn't matter how we got here. We need to work together to get to safety." He pushed at his door, but it didn't budge, and neither would hers.

The backseat windows weren't completely covered, so she unbuckled and crawled through the space between the front seats, well aware that her butt was in his face for most of her short trip. She lifted the door handle, and the door opened a few inches. She leaned back on her shoulders and pressed her heels to it. After several pushes, the door opened wide enough that she thought she could fit through it.

Her breath came in short, white bursts. "Maybe you should've done that."

"I wouldn't dare offer to help without being asked." That dimple of his made an appearance, so she did the only thing she could. She shimmied through the small space and crawled her way out of the car.

Ice slid down the back of her jacket in cooling surprise. Good. She needed a jolt to realize she couldn't feel this way about a man who entered her life a little over a week ago. A man all wrong for her. A man like the one she'd escaped from when she'd left the ranch after her mother's death. A man who haunted her until she'd found the right man—or so she'd thought—to marry.

A man who'd dropped a prenup on her wedding day.

Colt crawled out of the car, put gloves on, and tugged his jacket up around his throat. "Better get moving."

She should've remembered her thick gloves instead of the thin ones she'd slid on. The fashionable kind you wore from car to office, not from wreck to home.

The embankment challenged her resolve with each lift of a leg crunching above the knee in snow. Colt managed better with his height, but white puffs of smoke and his panting told her it was still a challenge.

For each few feet they climbed, they slipped and slid a few inches back. Halfway up, she found herself holding onto his arm. His strength and power weren't lost on her, but by the time they reached the top where they assumed the road existed, one thing was certain. Colt was right. They'd never make it back to the house. Not before they froze to death.

He took both her gloved hands in his and rubbed them. "You're freezing. Those are too thin."

"I'll be fine."

With one quick motion, he yanked his gloves from his hands and held them out, but she wouldn't take them.

"Stupidity deserves suffering."

"Wow, that's harsh. Who told you that?"

She averted her gaze, unable to share that she'd coined that phrase herself in the boardroom. "Doesn't matter."

A place existed not too far away that could be their saving grace, but she wouldn't go there. Couldn't go there. Could she?

She slid her cell phone from her pocket in a vain attempt to get a signal. Anything was better than that cabin only a half mile through some rugged terrain. A place she swore she'd never return to in this lifetime. But it wasn't just her life she risked.

"Maybe if we go to the clearing," he offered, but she knew better.

"No, but there's somewhere we can go." Her gut twisted and heart snapped in half like the branch that had sent them down a ravine. A ravine she should've stayed in, because returning to the hunting cabin was something she couldn't face. Not the memories or the lies from the day she discovered her high school sweetheart, Trevor, with another woman. The day of her mother's funeral.

Chapter Fifteen

THE SUN'S muted hues beyond the dark clouds warned that the temperature would be dropping faster than his father had excommunicated him from the family. He slid his cell phone out of his pocket.

Saige faced the tree line, and those unshed tears made another appearance. The way she clutched her coat to her chest and her chin dipped told him the place they were headed held something dark.

He couldn't stand to see her upset, so he reached high over his head with his cell in hopes he could reach a magical signal.

"Won't matter how tall you are. No service." She marched down the hill with pure determination to get them home.

He caught up and kept pace with her. The woman didn't stop. She hung a right and used a tree to pull herself a foot up a fifteen-foot hill. Bark broke, and she fell back into his arms. He grabbed her before she tumbled and hit her head on some unseen rock. "I know I risk being tossed off a ridge, but do you want to talk about it?"

She rested her head on his shoulder, the first sign her wall hadn't been completely reconstructed. She shivered in his arms, so he pulled her tight and rubbed her back, her hands folded between their bodies in those darn gloves.

Two deep, stuttered breaths later, she pushed from his arms. "Nothing. Just cold and tired."

He longed to know more, but why would this woman trust him with her secrets when he hadn't trusted her with his? Did she know he kept something from her? Maybe it was time to open his own life and share. "Do you want to know why I came out here?"

A tree creaked and wobbled, then fell into another one, which caused a branch to tumble to the ground reminding him they needed to stay focused, but they also needed a distraction from the cold and wet world around them.

Despite her lack of response, he continued. "I'm exactly what you accused me of being when we met—a lazy, no-good womanizer. I came out here to get away and try to figure out how to be a better man."

She stopped and bent over, hands to knees, for a break. "I don't see it."

Those few words opened the door to a conversation, and he entered. "What part?"

"You're anything but lazy. I'm a hard worker, and I have trouble keeping up with you." She shrugged and returned to her slow and steady climb.

"Let me guess. Dad wanted a star son, and you didn't live up to his expectations. Seen that story a few too many times." Her voice cracked. He wasn't sure if it was from the cold or emotion since he couldn't see her face. "Maybe you should stop trying to be what your father wanted and be who you were meant to be. You're happy when you're cooking and working with your hands."

"Can't make much money doing either of those. That would add to his disappointment." He inhaled an icy sting of a breath and turned the conversation on her. This was his opportunity to slip in his real life to her. "I'm not who I was meant to be. I need to face life and what waits for me. I was excommunicated from the family until I get my head on straight." He heard the heavy sadness in his own voice.

She spun around, mouth ajar with tiny puffs of steam evaporating inches from her face. Snow dotted her nose and chin and brows. She swiped it away and looked at him as if for the first time. "I can't imagine you did anything so terrible to deserve that."

"I dared to disobey his wishes."

The silence that only a good snowfall allowed made him realize they were the only two people in the world at that moment. And despite the cold, he didn't mind.

"What were his wishes?"

"To take over the family business, but I came out here instead."

"Just because you chose a different path doesn't mean you're not a good man. Trust me, it's harder to be your own person than bury yourself in your father's wishes. Who cares if you're broke if you've found something better than money." She grabbed a branch and took a short break. "Your father's a jerk if he can't see the man you've become because he's blinded by his own dreams."

He blinked at her, the only woman ever to dare say anything negative about his father. Of course, she didn't know who she was speaking about, but something told him it wouldn't matter if she did. This woman wouldn't bow down to his every order.

"Don't take offense. Mine is too. Unlike yours, though, mine wants me to be around him. More than that, to *be* him. It's better to live your truth than to live a lie. Lies are poison. Lies destroy people." She mumbled something under her breath he didn't catch, but when she hoofed it up the hill faster, he decided not to pry any further. They'd have all night, if they made it to shelter.

He needed tell her his truth. The woman thought he was a poor rancher who left a family business to pursue his dreams. Not the billionaire bad boy who shirked his responsibilities to enjoy life in his youth. She'd never respect that man. Did he even want to be that man anymore?

If only his father would've allowed him to join the Boy Scouts when he was younger. He'd said it was foolish nonsense because men like the Whitmores didn't need outdoor skills. They could pay someone to build a fire for them.

They reached the top of the hill to flat ground. He heaved and held on to a tree to catch his breath. "Guess...not...used...to...altitude."

She bent over, hands on knees, and nodded. "Not much farther."

"Good." Despite the heaviness in his chest, he managed to catch his breath and scan the flat ground and then up the next hill, where he saw a brown dot. "Please tell me it's not that."

"Fine. I won't tell you." She stood upright.

He was thankful for his new snow boots, the ones Saige bought for a man she thought was down on his luck, not a man with millions in his bank account. He didn't have the energy to get into that conversation, not to mention she might shove him down the mountain. A groan welled up inside him, and he let it out.

Howls responded in the distance, which urged him to get moving. "Don't want to be out here at night."

"No, we don't." She didn't move, though. Instead, she took a step into his space. "I'm truly sorry I got us into this. Maybe I am stubborn, but being a woman in the corporate world, I've had to be that way. I wish I could be more like you. Honest and gentle and kind."

His insides knotted with guilt. He cleared his throat and decided to stay on her topic for now. There would be plenty of time to talk once they reached the cabin. "Trust me, I understand. The thought of my baby sister having to face men who belittle her churns my stomach."

"You really love your sister." Her eyes lit up. "I always wished I had a sibling. I always envied my great-grandmother Francine for having six sisters. They were apparently beautiful, strong, smart, and successful. Of course, they all ended up separated in order to survive. It's a miracle they all made the trip and, to my understanding, all lived great lives."

"Sounds like you're from a line of strong women."

She offered a genuine smile that chased the frost from his insides for a moment. He took her by the elbow and walked to the next hill. She took his hand to pull herself up to the first tree.

"I had no idea how much I could care about another human until she came into my life. And to think, I was bitter about her birth."

"Because of your father and stepmother?" she asked.

He managed to grab hold of the next tree and hoist himself up the steep, slippery hill. "My father remarried too fast for my taste after the divorce. A month later, they announced they were having a baby. I spent seven months angry, unable to face my new insta-family. But then, when I held Abbey in the hospital, I realized she was an innocent in the drama of our lives. And I hate to admit it, but I saw a love in my father's eyes I'd never seen before. A love he'd never shown me. It made him seem human."

"I've never seen that in my father's eyes. Not since my mother died." She missed Colt's hand and fell on her hip with a thud. He was down on his knees by her side in a breath.

"You okay?"

She rubbed her backside. "Only bruised along with my ego. Despite all the Pilates and running I do, this hill is kicking my butt."

Wind blew the tall pines, making them arch as if to bow to Mother Nature, causing them to dump piles of snow down around them. A warning of foul weather ahead.

"Don't feel bad. This is killing me." He dusted the snow from her cheek. Another howl wrenched the air, so he helped her to stand. "Come on. We can do this together."

She held tight to him. "I'm feeling like I've been locked in a team-building exercise."

"Never did one of those. My father doesn't believe in teamwork. He believes in competition."

They clawed their way up several more feet and then sat for a short rest to catch their breath. "My father believes in conquering."

"Sounds like our fathers would get along. What was your mother like?"

Saige pushed from the ground without a word, telling him the topic of her mother was off-limits. To his relief, they reached the top of the hill and the cabin came into full view, with its tin roof, weathered wood exterior, and a single chimney.

"Doesn't look like much, but we can get a fire going and wait out the storm. Hopefully, the pipes aren't frozen so we can get some water."

He hoped he could get a fire going. "Guess I should warn you that my fire-building skills aren't up to par. Never made a fire without the right tools before."

"No worries. I can get a fire going in twenty seconds or less."

He quirked a brow at her. "Girl Scouts?"

"Brownie dropout, but trust me, I can do it."

"I have no doubt you can do anything you set your mind to."

Saige stood at the door but didn't move.

"Is it locked?" He reached around, but the door opened. The tiny, rundown cabin welcomed them inside. The small space meant fewer places for Saige to run and hide away from him. That being said, he hoped the structure would hold up to the incoming storm and the truth he needed to share.

They had a lot to talk about after her near meltdown at the restaurant. Something deeply troubled her.

The sparsely furnished cabin blocked the majority of the wind, but cool air gushed through small holes between wood slats. "That fire you were bragging about?"

She removed her gloves, revealing bright-red hands that matched her face. He removed his own gloves and rubbed life back into her hands, blowing on her skin in hopes of warming it.

Soft, tiny hands easily fit into his grasp. Her eyes slid shut, but then she jerked away. "Fire."

He didn't pursue her. He had all night to ease into finding out what put such distance between them suddenly. He lowered the wood slat to secure the door.

Saige wadded up some old newspapers, stuck them under a couple logs, and struck a match.

"Didn't think about the fact there might be matches or lighters in here."

"Don't underestimate us country folk. We always come prepared." She held her palms to the fire. "Well, except when we have temper tantrums and run off into a storm in a midsize sedan."

They both laughed and found a place to snuggle up next to the fire. Wind whistled outside like an angry wolf ready to blow the house down. "Need to take off our damp coats. I'll grab the blanket from the bed. Stay by the fire."

He took the dusty old blanket and shook off what he could and then returned to wrap it around her.

"You're shivering. Come on." She held up part of the blanket, and he joined her.

"Didn't want to be presumptuous."

"Freezing to death trumps personal space, especially when I'm at fault for the situation."

"Don't be so hard on yourself." He wrapped his arm around her and scooched her tight against him. His body responded, pulse tap, tap, tapping against his neck. The feeling of her nestled against him did something inside him. A strange, nervous twitch jumped in his stomach.

They sat in silence for a while, watching the flames until they began to dull and he got up to stir them back to life. She eyed the sink and two cabinets. "I'll see if there's any food or if the water works. Totally forgot about our salads in the car."

He threw another log on the fire and hoped they had enough from the pile in the corner for the night. Nothing outside would be dry enough at this point to light.

Several minutes later, she shook her head. "Water isn't on, and no lights. Found enough beef jerky to last us a couple weeks, a couple bags of chips, and a case of sodas, plus one gallon jug of water. A dinner of champions."

"Or desperate cabin squatters stranded in a snowstorm," he teased.

"That, too." She settled down, and they feasted on junk food and soda while watching the flickering light until she yawned and her eyes fluttered.

"You take the bed and blanket. I can stay by the fire and keep it going."

She eyed the bed, her lips tight, eyes wide. Those unshed tears made an appearance, but she blinked them away. "No. Not that bed."

"What's going on, Saige? You can tell me. Whose cabin is this? Did someone die here?" he asked.

"No, but someone should have," she said in a dull tone.

Chapter Sixteen

THE OLD LOG cabin with stone fireplace closed in on Saige with unwanted memories. Zaps of nerves shot through her the way they had the day she'd spotted Trevor with the skank in their special place. This cabin had been her refuge from her father's anger and her mother's illness. A place for the two of them, not a spot to invite another girl. Not on the day of her mother's funeral.

Colt's reassuring hand cupped her cheek. "Hey, it's okay. You don't have to tell me anything. We can stay right here next to the fire."

The warmth, the comfort of a strong man with a sensitive touch and sweet words, made her lean into his promise to be there for her. She closed her eyes and for a second believed all the nightmares of this place could be exorcised by this man at her side. But comfort was temporary. Men like Trevor or Colt, with their suave moves and strong bodies and confidence, never remained loyal. He'd said himself he wasn't a good man. But everything she'd seen and witnessed told her he was but couldn't see it in himself. No, she wouldn't fall into this trap again. Besides, she didn't deserve comfort, not when she'd lost a good man because she couldn't accept the dependable, honest, hardworking businessman. The safe partner in life. Her heart got in the way of what she should want—stability and partnership.

She pushed away and dropped the blanket to the ground, welcoming the cold of the night around her frozen heart. Strength came from within, not from someone else, so she marched to the bed, ready to shove out her own darkness. But with each step, her body trembled and her breath lodged somewhere between her lungs and her nightmare.

Trevor's dark suit and the girl's black dress tossed on the wooden floor. Saige could taste her salty tears, smell the sex and betrayal in the room. The moans and cries pierced her ears like an ice shoe climbing the mountain of betrayal. Trevor's gaze snapped to her standing like a statue, unable to look away.

Flash after flash of the memories of that day trampled her heart like a thousand wild stallions running over her.

The memories stuttered with darkness, but she knew there were more. More than she'd allowed herself to remember all these years, but then she saw it. His face, his eyes spying her, and a thin smile.

"He didn't stop."

"Who?" Colt's voice jolted her back. He rushed to her side, and she saw a look of horror on his face that told her he thought the worst. "You're safe now." He reached for her, but she retreated from his touch.

"I wasn't assaulted." She cleared her throat and blinked away the tears. "I'd vowed that day never to shed another tear, and I haven't. He wasn't worth it." She laughed. "I've never spoken about what happened to anyone. I thought I'd buried it, but maybe some things don't stay buried."

He gestured to the fire. "Maybe it's time you told someone. If you're worried about having anyone else know, you only hired me for two more weeks, so I'm a good confidant."

The way his face tightened with worry made her think this man cared. Really cared, as if he never wanted to see her hurt and would rather die than harm her. "Maybe we can extend your employment. You know, to see what possibilities turn up. If I ever get us out of this mess I've created." She shrugged, but her muscles ached either from the cold or from the memories; she wasn't sure.

He settled on the floor with the look of a little boy ready to roast marshmallows on a winter evening. She wasn't sure if it was because Colt had spent the last week with her and earned a morsel of her trust or because she couldn't make it through a night in this awful place without talking about it or because he'd proven himself a respectful man and a hard worker, but she yearned to share with him. She needed to share with someone because she hadn't had a life here since that night.

With a deep breath and a need to chase off the bone-deep chill, she returned to the fireside and faced Colt. She couldn't come up with the words at first, and he sat patiently for the longest time. The fire crackled. Wolves howled. Wind whistled.

He took the blanket and wrapped it around her. "You're shivering. I'd hold you tight and get you warm, but I think you need space."

How did he know what she needed when she didn't have a clue? "I guess it wouldn't hurt to tell you. It's not like it's a secret that could cause any real damage. I'm not sure why I've never told anyone, except I thought it was just something in my past. Honestly, I hadn't thought about Trevor since I left MH Ranch a decade ago."

She let out a half chuckle mixed with a half moan. "Almost to the day. My mother's funeral was ten years ago today."

"I'm so sorry. I can't imagine being a teenager and facing such pain." His words were soft and soothing, coaxing her to say more.

Saige clutched the blanket around her and eyed the bed. He followed her gaze but then tended the fire, stirring sparks that danced up into the chimney as if to escape this place the way she longed to.

"After the funeral, I came here. It had been Trevor's and my special place. I got in a fight with my father because he wanted me to move with him and leave the ranch. He said I was too much like my mother and needed to toughen up and it was time to live in the real world."

"Harsh. I'm not sure I like your father much more than I like my own. Funny how that is."

"What?" she asked, welcoming the distraction for a second to gather her strength to face what came next.

"We can love our parents, but sometimes we don't like them." He chuckled, and she knew he remembered the argument that drove him from his family.

"Why did your father disown you?" she asked.

He scrubbed his stubbled jaw. "I want to tell you. I *need* to tell you, but this isn't about me right now. Maybe tomorrow we'll discuss why I'm here. Tonight, in this place... This is about you."

Since when did anyone in her life ask how she was? Thomas had been there for all the important decisions, but he wasn't an affectionate person. They never spoke about feelings. "Alright. Tomorrow you'll share your story."

He nodded, but the way his shoulders rose to his ears told her it would be difficult for him.

She toyed with a frayed edge of the blanket. The same blanket that had been on the bed all those years ago. Did he still come to this place? She shoved the thought from her mind. "After the funeral, I came here to get away, but I heard something inside." She swallowed the lump rising in her throat. No tears. Never again. Not for him. "He was inside, but something told me not to open the door." She lifted her hand as if to reach for the knob, the vision pounding her head with no restraint. "I turned it, and the door creaked open. The sounds intensified. Animalistic, raw sounds. My knees were weak and I thought I'd collapse, but I stepped inside."

She dropped her hand and shook off the memory for a second to take a sip of water. "Funny part is that my mother and my friends warned me about him, but I was too in love to see it. They'd said a guy like him would never be here for a girl like me. My father said he wanted my family money. He was the partying type, the kind who runs off in the middle of the night or lets you down at the worst moment of your life."

He closed his eyes, and the lines deepened around his mouth. "I know the type."

Did he have a woman in his past who had done something to him? Maybe this would help him open up. Maybe he wasn't one of those kinds of men. Maybe she could change him the way she thought she could change Trevor. Stupid. These kinds of men always made women believe stupid lies.

She twisted the top onto the bottle and slipped back into the awful truth of this place. "The bed creaked and banged against the wall. I forced my gaze to go from my black leather boots, across the floor, up the bedpost, to this blanket." She held it open and wished she had another option so she could throw this one into the fire. "This blanket that entangled Trevor and another woman in our special place on the night of my mother's funeral. And do you know what he did?"

Colt shook his head as if not wanting to say anything in fear of her reaction. Smart man.

"He looked at me. That's it."

"What?" Colt's brow furrowed.

"No, he didn't just look at me. He smiled and kept going at it with the other woman as if I stood there as the audience for his great performance." Her voice cracked, but she cleared her throat and forced the pain down.

"I'm so sorry. What a monster." Colt scooted closer, but she put her palm up. No way she'd fall into another man's empty promises. "I hadn't realized it before, but Thomas was safe all this time. A man who spoke about decisions, never about feelings. Unlike a man of passion who fills the need for intimacy, but with that, brings the danger of heartbreak. To give another person the ability to crush you with one act, one word, one lie was something I couldn't do again. But in the end, I couldn't marry a man who wanted a sterile, emotionless life. I wanted what Francine and Walt had."

"I understand now," he mumbled but averted his gaze to the fire.

"Understand what?" she asked.

He glanced at the bed and then at her. "Why you can't let me in. Why you want something one minute from me but push me away the next. You see me as that man." He shuffled away.

"And you're right. You shouldn't be close to me. You deserve so much better."

She snagged his pinky. "You're too hard on yourself. Stop seeing yourself through your father's eyes. That kind of man wouldn't be next to me night after night this past week without trying to push things further than cuddling and hand-holding."

"You're right, I'm not Trevor. I can safely say I've never done anything like that. I've never intentionally hurt a woman, and I've never cheated on one. That man is the type who makes every other man look like a jerk. Now I see why you returned and why you couldn't be around your father. But that doesn't mean I'm a good man."

The fire popped, and a spark flew out onto the blanket. He reacted faster than a raccoon after a morsel of food in winter, smacking the flame into submission.

She looked at him, really looked at him. A man who didn't judge her, who worked hard, and who made a vow he'd never be like Trevor.

"Why do you think I couldn't be around my father?"

"Because you left here after this happened, the day after your mother's funeral, to a life you didn't originally want. You've made comments about how amazing your mother was. How you admired your great-great-great-great-grandmother Francine. You're back here hoping to find the person you lost that day."

Her mouth fell open. How could he decipher something in five minutes she couldn't figure out in a decade, and how did he remember how many greats to her grandmother? He'd paid attention. Trevor had never even remembered her birthday. Maybe a man did exist who offered both goodness and passion. "Okay, Dr. Colt, what do I do now?"

"You face the past and open yourself up to future possibilities." His words were simple, but when he took her hand in his and kissed her knuckles, his actions were complicated. Too complicated and dangerous.

"I vowed that day never to let a man have that kind of hold over me."

"You were young, and something tells me you're way too strong to ever let someone control you at this point in your life."

She chuckled. "Well, Dr. Colt, you psychoanalyzed part of it, but not all of it. My father's been controlling me for years, and he's not a man easy to refuse. I came all this way out here to get away from him so that I could learn to think for myself again. To reconnect with the McKinnie sisters. The last thing I need is another man in my life." Her pulse thudded a desire to return to their evening position by the fire and take it to the next step, but she couldn't. A part of her wanted to get back at Trevor by sleeping with another man in this place, but that was too juvenile, and she wouldn't do that to Colt. He deserved better. Even so, could she really trust a man like him with her heart? "Tomorrow you'll tell me your story, and then I can over-analyze you. After that, we'll discuss an extension of your employment or I'll send you packing."

He folded his arms over his chest and faced the fire. "Then I'm glad we have now."

His words sent a frost over her more fierce than the world outside. Whatever he had to share, it bothered him. Did he think it would change her mind about him? That she'd send him away because of some past mistake? Isn't that what she'd just said? "Listen, there are mistakes people make that are just that, mistakes. And then there are evil, selfish, and self-serving acts that degrade or humiliate someone. I won't turn my back because of a mistake. We all make them. I know I have. It's the deceit and the lies I can't handle. There's nothing worse than a liar who manipulates people."

She dared to approach, wanting to feel that connection with Colt again that she'd lost since entering this awful place. "Maybe it's time for us both to face our fears."

His hand covered hers on his shoulder. "What then? Facing fears is one thing. Making a change is far more difficult. I want to be the passionate, kindhearted man you see in me, but I'm not him. What if I can never be him?"

"Then we walk away forever."

Chapter Seventeen

COLT HATED himself for allowing Saige to assume things about him that weren't true. He hadn't *technically* lied, but he wasn't sure she'd see it that way.

But this man—Trevor—he made all men look bad in Saige's eyes. He'd face her and the truth he'd share tomorrow.

Ten years... That was a long time to hold on to that kind of pain. "I'm sorry we came here. If I'd known..."

"No." She sniffled, but as she'd vowed, not one tear slid down her rosy cheeks. The color had returned now that they were only chilly, not frozen. "I own my mistakes, and rushing out of the diner the way I did to usher you out of my life is on me." She crossed her legs and scooted closer to the fire. "This was the right choice for shelter. The only choice."

He scooted closer under the guise of wanting more warmth, but he wanted to feel that connection again. The one when she'd leaned into him. Her cheek pressed to his chest. He'd never felt this kind of flutter in his stomach and desire to feel closer beyond the physical need. "I don't mean to pry, but you said you left after you realized you couldn't marry Thomas, and that's why you went to your childhood ranch."

She picked up some kindling by her side, snapped it in half, and tossed it into the fire. "Yeah, that's true. What I didn't realize until I came to this shack is that our breakup was almost entirely my fault."

The kindling snapped and was engulfed by a hungry flame. "That's big of you. It takes two to make a relationship work."

"Maybe." She snapped another piece of kindling and tossed it into the blaze. "Was I stupid for giving up a dependable man because I wanted something that hasn't existed since the 1870s? Thomas isn't a bad man, but he cared more about money and position than a relationship. He'd been safe, but I know now I'm not only my father's child who cares only for money—as a matter of fact, I don't want a man with a big fortune and who cares more about taking over companies than the people who work for him. But I'm also not completely my mother's child because I can't blindly love someone who isn't there for me emotionally."

The way her gaze remained zoned in on the burning wood, her mouth ajar and her shoulders slumped, there was more to this perfect person. "But?"

"But he was right." She dusted her hands off and pulled the blanket tighter as if shielding herself from the mess of the world. "I didn't love Thomas. I was coldhearted and only cared about the next big deal. I don't want to be that person anymore. There has to be more to life."

"That's why you wanted to know more about the McKinnie sisters."

"Yes, but all I've discovered is a great love where the man chose to chase down a criminal instead of remaining by his wife's side." She held her palms out to the fire. "I'm a business shark and don't need a fictitious man to love me, one who will only disappoint me or lie to me later. A playboy or a rich man. The only thing that could be worse is a playboy rich man." She chuckled.

He swallowed hard, realizing the irony of his choice to join the Billionaire Bad Boys Club. She wouldn't want to be in the same room with him if he revealed that poor choice.

"Even if that were true, which I doubt it is, there're men out there who are both kind and strong-willed. A man who can appreciate a woman who knows what she wants and goes after it. A woman who stands up to men in the boardroom and puts them in their place, yet still has a soft heart for the man at home."

"In my experience, there are the men who are all passion and no commitment and those who are all commitment with no passion. I can live peacefully or face a man in bed with another woman again."

His chest tightened at the way her voice cracked each time she spoke about that day. A day that had obviously haunted her all these years.

His stepmother had made it seem like his father had been faithful since they married, that his extracurricular marital activities were because he didn't love his wife. Did that mean if Colt found the right woman, he'd never cheat on her? "It sounds like you've gone for extremes. Maybe it's time to try dating someone in the middle. A man who's kind yet strong. A man not threatened by your ability to take down a room full of businessmen but who wants to bring you flowers to celebrate your win."

"There isn't a man like that. Not that I've met."

"You haven't met all the men in the world." He nudged her

to think of him beyond the friend with possibilities who lived in her house. A dangerous game when he wasn't sure he could be that man and he'd never want to hurt her the way Trevor had. "I'm not going to argue the point that men don't screw up. They do. But there are the kind who make mistakes, learn from them, and try to make them right. And those who make mistakes and hide from them."

"Like partying and destroying a girl's place, then helping to clean it up?" she teased. "A wannabe cowboy who doesn't have plans for his future? A guy like you?"

He shrank from her words. "No, not like me. Better. You deserve better."

She ran her fingers through his hair in a dangerously provocative and promising way that challenged his better side. "Maybe you're exactly that man. You just don't know it yet."

She yawned. Exhaustion from the day took hold of him as well. They were too tired to dig into anything deeper tonight. He eyed the bed, but when she stiffened, he knew she'd never crawl up there. The thick carpet and pallet they'd made in front of the fire at the ranch, he could sleep on, but this hard floor would prove too difficult, not to mention the cold would chill them to the bone.

With a deep breath, he decided to try to prove he was a man of action but with a sensitive touch. He only hoped it didn't backfire. He pushed from the ground, stripped the bed, flipped the mattress, and plopped it down in front of the fire. She scooted away, but he knew Saige would never back down from a fight. "You can keep running from that moment, or you can face it now and move forward with your life. Make new memories to overshadow the old ones." He winked. "Besides, it's getting uncomfortable on the hard floor, the fire'll keep us warm, and we'll need rest if we're going to make the hike back to the house once the storm clears."

She blinked up at him, and he could see a hundred thoughts flash through her head in a few seconds. They'd spent several nights in front of the fire at her place on the carpet floor reclining against a couch and cuddled up, but this was different. A bed. A bed her ex had cheated on.

"I'll be a perfect gentleman, but the temperature's dropping, you're shivering, and if your back feels like mine, you're done with sitting on the floor." He stood and waited for her answer.

She quirked a brow at him. "Wouldn't a bad boy convince a woman to crawl into bed with him under the guise of keeping her warm?"

"I'm a recovering bad boy." He held up two fingers. "Scout's honor. I vow to keep my hands to myself." There. That would show her he was going to be a perfect gentleman. A man who could master his thoughts. He hoped. Because standing over the mattress with a romantic fire and a beautiful woman? Not a fair test for any man.

"You're no Boy Scout, so don't try to pretend to be one." She eyed the mattress but then crawled up on it and fluffed the blanket out to cover both sides of the bed before pulling a corner back.

He didn't need any further invitation, so he joined her with an inch between them, not wanting to spook her. "What gave me away?"

"It's three fingers, not two." She rolled over to face the fire, so he chose to remain on his back, eyeing the roof, thankful it was sloped and made of tin, or this could be a different story.

"Busted." He chuckled. "Doesn't mean I don't want to be a good guy, though."

"Really? Then what are the thoughts in your head right now?" she asked in a teasing tone.

"As I said, you need a bad boy who behaves like a gentleman."

She reached back and grabbed his hand, tugging him to roll over to spoon with her and wrapping his arm tightly around her. "Then let's hope the gentleman in you doesn't give way to the dark side, because as you said, we need to stay warm."

He cleared his throat and attempted to clear his mind of all the thoughts racing through his head while alone in a cabin with a beautiful woman pressed against him. Talk about a rigged test. If he was going to suffer all night with want and need, he decided to let his devilish side peer out, if only for a second. What could she do? Run out into the snow to escape him?

He settled in closer and rested his mouth to her ear. "No need to worry about warmth, because the mere thought of what could be between you and my less-tamed side is enough to keep me hot all night."

Chapter Eighteen

MEMORIES OF TREVOR faded into the darkness while images of Colt danced in the light of the flames in front of Saige.

When was the last time her body woke to the point of pure desire? Not in this place. Not with a man who couldn't be real.

"Relax. I told you I'd be good." He pressed a sweet kiss to her temple, but her body didn't respond with the same innocence. She kicked one foot out from the covers to chill her body once more into submission, but she wasn't sure dancing naked in the snow could cool her want.

To her relief, he got up to stoke the fire to allow hers to burn out to glowing embers. A few sips of water and a stretch made the situation a little more bearable. How come her body hadn't responded to Thomas's touch this way? No man ever drove her to the point of being unable to control herself. That deep need for connection, fulfillment, satisfaction. Not since Trevor.

All the more reason to see Colt for who he was. A guy who would stir her up and spit her out, even if he didn't mean to.

She knew the cowboy types. They changed directions with the wind.

That cooled her libido, and she allowed herself to fall into a fitful sleep until the first rays of light shone through the window.

Warm and safe, she snuggled into the blanket and the hard body at her back before she remembered where she was and who she was with.

"Shh, relax." He stroked her hair away from her face, leaving behind delicious tingles radiating through her scalp and down the nape of her neck. "I think I've proven my word's good. To you and to myself."

His hand drifted down to her shoulder, along her arm, and then his fingers laced between hers where her hand rested on her hip. This was wrong. Maybe she was the bad girl. What kind of woman wanted a man a week after she was supposed to exchange vows with another man?

How could she think about how Colt's lips would feel against hers? Enjoy the simple touch of his fingers along her skin? Take comfort in his arms during a raging storm outside? A man who chased away the haunts of her past and gave her hope of future possibilities.

Her breath came in rapid, chest-lifting bursts. His lips raked along her ear, and he pressed a kiss to her neck. "Your heart's beating fast and your breath is quick. If I'm reading the signs correctly, I best go check outside and put some space between us. Because despite my word, if you gave me reason to believe you wanted me to kiss you, I wouldn't be able to keep my promise."

He lifted the blanket and moved away. A rush of cold air

invaded her heat and calmed her pulse before her heart beat so hard it broke through her armor.

With deep breaths, she tended the fire, reviving it to a full blaze. The door opened behind her, and damp air saturated the room. She rushed back under the covers before the door shut and closed her eyes to face that awful day in this cabin now that she'd spoken about it. But instead of seeing Trevor on the bed, she saw Colt kissing her, and she couldn't help but think. Could this man possess the passion she craved with the touch and attention of an attentive partner?

She threw off the covers and decided to find out. A kiss. One kiss. It could be simple yet revealing. After all, she'd gone to the ranch to figure out what she wanted out of life, not close herself off from it.

Maybe Colt was right and he was a man who could have a wild streak but be a loving and honest person.

She went to the window and saw him trudging through the snow. A million thoughts went through her head, and she held on to the small table, eyeing the bed with no mattress and then the mattress by the fire.

The door swung open, and he slammed it shut but didn't secure it with the board. "Storm's gone. Sun's coming up. I found a shovel outside. Maybe we can dig the car out?" He shook off his jacket and hung it on the hook and then faced her. "What?"

She tried to share her thoughts, tell him what she was thinking, but her brain didn't slow long enough for her to catch a single thought, so she let go of the table and took a step toward a chance on something. The first risk she'd taken in a long time.

His eyes blazed with understanding, and he stood there as if waiting for her invitation, for her to tell him it was okay to kiss her, but she couldn't find the words, so she decided to show him. With pulse pounding, heart thumping, she closed the distance between them.

A revving in the distance told her there was a car on the road that could possibly rescue them from another night stuck in this cabin, but she didn't even look away. How could she, with Colt waiting for her next move?

"Are you sure?" he asked in a hoarse whisper.

"No," she managed but didn't stop her approach.

In one swift move, he had her in his arms and unleashed all the passion he'd been holding. It wasn't tentative like Thomas. It wasn't demanding like Trevor. It was desire and want and lust and need but with a hint of tenderness.

The floor disappeared from under her feet. She floated, his arms wrapped around her as he lifted her onto the small table and slipped his hands behind her neck, tilting her head and deepening the kiss. An avalanche of room-spinning, heart-pounding, unleashed need drove her to pull him even tighter, and she never wanted to let go.

In that moment, she thought nothing on this earth could ever tear them apart. A bond seared between them, and she wanted more, so much more. She wanted all the possibilities.

Chapter Nineteen

COLT'S MIND blurred into a whirl of want. Never had he ever needed a woman so bad in his life. Was this love? His body awoke and his heart thundered. With each swipe of a tongue, slide of her fingers along his neck, press of her body to his, he thought he'd never recover or be able to let Saige McKinnie out of his life.

She would *be* his life.

He had to stop this now, though, but how could he end a moment that felt like it started the rest of his life? This woman, she drew out his desire to be a better man. A man worthy of her love. And he could only earn that by telling the truth, so with painful effort, he lightened the kiss and nibbled her sweet lips for several minutes, along her jawline, ear, neck. "I have to tell you something, but I need you to know that I've changed—or you've changed me. I see the world in a different way."

She clawed at his shirt and lifted her chin, inviting him to continue his exploration, and he wanted to more than anything. But if he didn't tell her the truth, they could never have a future, and in this moment, the only future he saw had Saige in it.

The engine sound came closer, but he didn't care. He continued his trek down her neck to her collarbone. "I might have been a Thomas and a Trevor at points in my life, but I want to be Colt, a man who would never hurt you. Will cherish you. And more than anything, I want to get to know you better."

He was starved for more of her, but he stopped and stood straight, looking directly in her eyes. "I want to find out what possibilities exist between us, and I want to be a man worthy of your love." His voice cracked, and her hands were cupping his face, giving him comfort he didn't deserve.

Before he could say anything, she kissed him again. A soft, reassuring kiss. "I can't picture you saying anything that would be so horrible. I've made too many mistakes of my own to judge yours."

As she claimed his lips, he believed her, that she could forgive him, and that only made him want her more.

The roar of the engine drew closer. She froze in his arms.

"I'm sorry. Did I—"

"No. That's a snowmobile."

The engine grew louder and then cut off outside close to the cabin. He wanted to chase their rescuer away. He could have lived on this feeling with Saige for days with no food or water.

"Hello? Who's in there?" a voice called.

Saige stiffened and trembled. He held her up and eyed the unlocked door that swung open, startling him into a fighting stance. A man, about two inches shorter but with a true cowboy image from hat to boots, stood in the doorway with his gaze zoomed in on Saige.

Colt didn't like it, not one bit, so he stepped into the man's line of view and cleared his throat. "What do you want?" he said in his deepest, I-can-take-you tone.

"Someone reported smoke over the radio, so I came to see who was in my cabin." He shifted to the side and narrowed his eyes. "Saige? That you?"

Colt calculated all the factors. This man's claim on the cabin, Saige's wide eyes and trembling lip, the man's hungry gaze on her. He didn't like how it all added up. "We didn't mean or want to be here, I assure you."

Saige put a hand to his chest and looked up at him. "It's okay. I've got this." She straightened herself to her shotgun pose and took two steps toward the man who'd crushed her all those years ago. The man Colt wanted to crush at this moment.

"My car ended up in the embankment. We had no choice but to hike up here for shelter during the storm. We'll be heading back to the car to dig it out shortly."

"City life make you forget about the roads 'round here? What were you doing driving in the storm?"

Saige hesitated, so Colt jumped in. "My fault. I needed to get back to the ranch to get to work."

"Well, you're not going to dig your car out with that." The man removed his hat and brushed his light hair back from his face then returned the large-brimmed hat to his head. "I'll radio in. You can ride down with me. Sorry. Only room for one." He eyed Colt, daring him to challenge his offer.

Colt took the proverbial glove he threw down and moved to accept, but Saige regained her words and said, "I'll walk, but if you can call in for a plow, that would be great."

Her words were sincere, tone direct, and body tense, but

Colt saw it. She touched her cowboy charm, and he knew the truth, that she was struggling to maintain her composure.

He couldn't help but jump in. "Since we crashed here for the night, we'll straighten up the cabin and then head down and meet the crew to get the car out. I'm happy to pay for any service that can help dig us out."

"Big spender, huh?" Trevor asked in an insulting tone.

"More like a man who cleans up after he makes a mess of someone's life."

"Go, Trevor." Saige tossed the blanket from her shoulders. "The hike down will be much easier than the hike up. Request a pass of the salt truck."

"I'll make sure the road's clear to town." Trevor tipped his hat and spun on his boots.

Colt couldn't let it go. He wanted to send the smug man tumbling down the mountain, but if there was one thing he saw that could hit the man without landing Colt in jail, it was the way he looked at Saige. The way a man looked when he wanted something from a woman. "No need. I'll be returning to MH Ranch with Saige."

Trevor paused at the open door, allowing the cold air to flood into the cabin. "Saige?"

She glanced at Colt, and he offered a nod. "She's in good hands. The softer kind." He winked. "It'll be easier for the salt truck to clear to the house anyway."

"But there's another storm heading this way. You could be stuck there for days with this…this…"

"Colt. And that won't be a problem. It'll be a pleasure," she said without missing a beat, as if she'd recovered from the shock of seeing the man who'd broken her into pieces she still needed to put back together.

Trevor stepped outside. "I'll have the salt truck clear the road from your house to town in case you have a change of heart."

"No, my heart is clear for the first time." Saige didn't move, not even a muscle twitch. Colt feared she didn't even breathe until the door closed behind Trevor and she crumbled against the table, heaving in stuttered breaths.

Colt took her into his arms and held her tight. "I don't know that I have the right to say this, but I'm proud of you. You're one of the strongest women I know."

She trembled in his arms, and he knew it was more from emotion than cold, but he retrieved the blanket and pulled her into his side to stand in front of the fire while he rubbed circles on her back.

"I haven't allowed myself to feel anything for so long, and now my chest feels like I have a decade of garbage crushing my ribs. I'm not sure I like this feeling. Being closed off to the world has worked well for me. Well, until I faced marriage to a man as closed off as I was."

"Stop blaming yourself. Be grateful that you saw the truth and walked out before it was too late.

"Too late?" She tossed the blanket off and took the poker to the fire, beating the wood until it fell apart into glowing embers. "I think the day of your wedding is too late. I'm tired of living a lie. It's time for me to face all my ghosts. That's why I came here, to reconnect with my past, my mother, and the rest of the McKinnie family. I've let a worthless playboy own too much of my life. I'll never let a man like him near me again."

Colt needed more time to prove he wasn't that guy. Besides, he wasn't going to leave her alone with that Trevor character.

His truth would wait until they were back at the ranch and Trevor was gone.

Saige returned the poker but remained focused on the fading glow of the debris. "Hey, I have an idea. I know I need to return soon, but there's no need before Christmas since the offices shut down. Since you have nowhere you need to be and I'll be off, we should both stay through Christmas. I don't think either one of us wants to head back to our lives before then, so why don't we stay at the ranch until the new year?"

"I think I'd like that."

The sound of the snowmobile fading away drew her attention to the window. "I could pay you extra, of course."

A jolt of hurt shot through him. "This isn't about a job anymore."

"I insist." She didn't look at him, only toyed with her charm, distracting him with the memory of kissing her and how they were about to take a step in the right direction before Cowboy Trevor interrupted. He didn't know the guy, but he didn't like him.

"Fine. If that's how you want to name this, then I'll work for room and board." He grabbed the mattress and tossed it on the bed and then grabbed their coats. Irritation built up inside him. He wanted to give her space to figure things out, but making him feel like her prostitute cowboy didn't sit well with him.

"After the next storm and the roads clear, I'll take you back to town." She slid her arms into the coat he held up for her. "I'm sorry. I didn't mean to offend you. It's just that..."

"It's fine," he grunted.

She spun to face him and clutched his coat. "I want you to stay. Not because I'm paying you but because I want to get to know you better. I fell back on money and power to protect my heart, but I don't want to do that anymore. From this moment forward, you're not my employee, you're my guest. Although, if you decide to leave after Christmas, I'll give you the money since you'll need it to figure out what's next in your life. I don't care if you're poor. Actually, I like that because I don't have to compete with you in business or come home to a sterile life. I like that you're all free and wild, which is my problem. Maybe you're right, though, and you could be both passionate and good."

He couldn't tell her that he didn't need the money, that he had plenty in an account with his name on it that he refused to touch.

"Tell me you forgive me. I'm sorry. My emotions are all over the place. I've protected myself for so long I don't know how to truly trust anyone again." She stood up on her tiptoes and tugged him down, her lips close enough to feel her breath on his mouth.

"Forgiven." He nuzzled her neck and kissed her cheek, the corner of her lip, but stopped because he knew that Trevor fellow would interrupt them if he took it any further, and he wanted to wait until they were alone to show her how he really felt about her. He wanted more from her, more of what she'd given him a moment before Trevor walked into the cabin, and if they were going to take this any further, he wanted to tell her the truth, so he tore himself away and headed outside.

Thank goodness the icy air cooled his body, or it would've been a difficult promise to keep. He took her hand, and they slushed and slipped down the hill until they spotted a big truck pulling her car out, and Colt knew before he saw the cowboy get out of his car that it was Trevor. The dark antihero of Saige's story.

Colt squeezed her hand tighter in fear she'd release his when they approached, but she didn't. She held tight all the way to her car and even leaned into Colt when they reached Trevor. "I appreciate you pulling my car out."

"Loaded up your stuff in the back. Salt truck can't get here until later today. I'll give you a ride back. You can't get there in this death trap."

Colt eyed the two-seater truck and knew where Trevor was headed with this offer. But Colt would flip it on him. "I'll hike back up later but appreciate the ride. I'm sure Saige can fit on my lap." He led her to the passenger side and crawled up into the cab. Then he helped Saige onto his lap.

Trevor detached her car and climbed into the truck. "You sure you want to hike back up here? It could be dangerous. We wouldn't want you falling off the side of a mountain. This country's rugged."

"You're right. Good thing I'm a former Boy Scout."

Saige's ribs vibrated, and he knew she was stifling a laugh. Colt tugged her closer and then strung the seat belt over the both of them. "Better to be safe."

She put her hand behind his neck and leaned into him. Her fingers toyed with his hair, and he realized she tamed him with a simple touch. How he'd love to be her cowboy, if only for Christmas.

Chapter Twenty

SAIGE SAT SILENTLY WATCHING the trees pass one by one. Images of that day, the worst day of her life, bombarded her. Out of all the people to waltz back into her life, it had to be Trevor. Apparently, facing the memories of their cabin wasn't enough. She had to face him again.

Not that it should've been a surprise, since his family owned the cabin, but still. Talk about being smacked by the past.

On the tight turn at the bottom of the hill, she had to admit Trevor knew this land and how to expertly navigate it. Her insides churned like she rode the snowplow over rugged terrain instead of a four-wheel-drive truck down a hill.

"So what have you been up to?" Trevor asked as if they were old friends meeting for afternoon tea.

Saige cuddled into Colt even more, realizing she was actually leaning on a man for support, literally and emotionally. He was her home base in this feelings game of hide and seek. How many times had she thought of what she'd say to the man who destroyed her completely? Yet, now, she couldn't even think, so she blurted her resume instead. "I'm a CEO."

Pride filled her. She wanted him to know that his betrayal didn't matter, that she'd succeeded in spite of it. Colt did that small circle thing on her back, easing her tension.

"No surprise. Your father always told me you'd succeed if I were out of your life."

Did her father chase him away? Is that what happened? Didn't matter. He hadn't chased Trevor into the arms of another woman. "How's your riding going? Bull riding, I mean."

She caught a slight grin on Colt's face and knew he was cheering for her. She liked that about him. Maybe there could be something beyond the physical draw between them. Keeping him around through Christmas, only to see him leave, would be difficult considering how much her body responded to a simple glance, touch…kiss.

What had that gotten her last time? A broken heart and a right fork on the road of life.

The truck grumbled at the next turn, and from the higher vantage point, she could see over the snow embankment and realized she'd risked not only her life but Colt's. The life of a man who held her protectively. A hero who wanted to defend her honor, despite only knowing her for a short time. That's what he'd be in a rom-com anyway. But this wasn't a movie. This was her life.

Trevor turned onto the main road, and she couldn't help but feel the symbolism to her life. Maybe she could still find her way back onto her true path. A path she knew meant fitting her mother's ranch into her life somehow.

"Glad you were able to reach our cabin. You would've died out there overnight."

"*Your* cabin. And it was a last resort, I assure you." She

didn't like the way her voice wavered. CEOs didn't show weakness to the enemy. Maybe channeling her father wasn't so bad in this moment. Could she be what Colt saw in her, a woman of strength and compassion?

Facing the most horrible experience of her life with him had made an impossible and difficult situation bearable. More than that. Her lips tingled with the thought of their kiss.

If Trevor hadn't shown, what would've happened? Something wild fluttered in her belly.

Trevor kept glancing over at her as if to construct the right thing to say, but what could he say? Nothing could change the way she felt about him. Ever.

Around the bend, the house came into view farther up the road. A beacon in the wild land of snow and trees. "Looks rundown. I'll come 'round when the snow thaws and help with some work."

"No need. I'll be working on things now," Colt announced with an authoritative tone.

Trevor scratched his chin, tipped his hat up, and eyed Colt. "No offense, but you don't look like the heavy-lifting, dirty-job kind of guy."

"A man can be a gentleman and still handle himself in rugged situations." Colt tightened his arms around her in a protective, I've-got-you kind of way.

"We grew up together, and I spent time on this ranch. We have history."

Saige felt his muscles tense behind his neck and decided this needed to end now. "I'm sure you have more important things to do than come out here to work on the ranch. Colt and I have it covered. It's time for me to focus on my future."

He turned up the driveway and focused forward. "Always thought I'd run this place one day."

Something told her that he had more to say, but he rolled to a stop without a word.

Colt opened the door before the tires stopped. "I'm sure Saige is capable of running her own ranch now that she's back." He retrieved the bags out of the back, including groceries and a few tools.

She stood on the icy ground, but the way Trevor looked at her made her blood boil. Not because he stoked the fire inside her with want but because he lit up at the idea she'd be staying, which meant he'd be back. And she didn't want him back. Not here, not now, not ever. Before she had a chance to tell him as much, Colt slammed the truck door, took her by the hand, and escorted her to the front porch.

Trevor didn't let it go, though. He rolled down his window and shouted, "I'll check on you tomorrow." He patted the side of his truck and scanned the barn. "Too bad you don't have horses no more. Not really a ranch now, huh?"

His words gutted her. After all these years, how did he still know how to hit her point blank in the heart from hundreds of yards away while galloping through the woods?

The wheels crunched over the ice the way his words crunched her heart. "My mother would be devastated at the sight of this place. No cows or horses or dogs or people to call this place home. Home and family. The McKinnie way of life for generations."

Colt ushered her inside, shut the door behind them, dropped the bags, and was at her side, cupping her face with his large hands. "We'll fix this place together. Not because I think you can't do it alone, but because I want to help. I love this place. It feels like home like no other house I've ever lived in." He locked the door and put his hands on her hips, his eyes soft but wide. "You're one amazing woman. Brave and composed. You did it. You faced your worst nightmare and survived."

Part of her wanted to fall into his arms and allow him to chase away the nightmares of her past, but the other part of her told her to back away and breathe. Life had been so tumultuous in recent days, she needed time to sort through everything. "I need a drink."

She removed her coat and hung it on the hook before crossing her arms over her chest, wanting to give him attitude, but also wanting to make sure she kept her hands to herself.

"How about some food in our bellies before that." He hung his coat by hers, ran a hand through his hair, grabbed the bags, dropped them in the kitchen, and headed down the hall. "If you need anything, I'm here. I'm happy to listen."

"I'm fine. Better than I thought I'd be. Although, I'd be happier if he was cursed with premature baldness or had a beer gut and missing teeth."

"Ouch, harsh. Remind me never to get on your bad side." He took a right turn into the grand room, and as if he'd taken an advanced course on fire building, flames erupted in a matter of seconds.

The man kept her warm, defended her honor, and made fire. What else could she want? He was perfect. Too perfect. Men like him didn't exist. Not since the 1870s.

She eyed her great-grandmother Francine's book and decided to flip through a few more of the legible pages. She curled up next to the fire. "I think I can read these pages. You want to hear more from Francine and Walter's world?"

Colt leaned around the corner with his bright smile. "Yeah, love to."

She moved to the kitchen with him, sat at the bar, and cleared her throat.

"I sit by the fire with Kerrie and Lucas by my feet, attempting to appear calm, but the pains have come on and the snow is so fierce that I can't imagine Walt making it home in time. I'm alone, but I know what to do after birthing two already. I long for one of my sisters to walk through that door in time, but I can't count on such miracles."

The writing smeared for a few lines, so she flipped the page.

"The pains are closer, and I know by morning I'll have a babe in my arms. I can't help but fear the worst has happened to my dear Walt. After losing my brothers and parents to the Civil War, my mind can't help but slip to violence and murder. The wind is whipping outside in warning, and I know the snowfall is coming. I thought about trying to make it to another ranch, but I won't risk Kerrie and Lucas."

She paused and skimmed through more faded writing, straining to make out the words.

"That is one brave woman. I can't imagine being alone here, about to have a child. Do you know who you're related to? Could you be the great-great-great-granddaughter of Kerrie or Lucas or the baby?"

A sense of belonging bubbled up inside her. "Wait a second... I remember something my mother said about the naming traditions. In honor of the seven sisters and three brothers, Francine continued the letter naming tradition. Each child named with the next letter of the alphabet. I'm Saige, my mother Rosemary, and my grandmother was Quinn. I remember because I thought it was an unusual name for a woman. I think my great-grandmother's name was something like Pauline or Pollyanna. I don't know who was before her, but if it is straight down the female line, I could be related to Kerrie."

"Unless the baby is a girl."

"Right." Excitement filled her with this family tree puzzle. She flipped the page and read further, but there were only bits and pieces. "Wait. I think I found something. Walt. Yes, I think he made it home."

Colt joined her, wielding a spatula. "What does it say?"

"I can't make it all out, but here it says, *I see him riding toward me. His hat covering his eyes, blocking the light snow falling to his face.*"

"Then what? Is the *him* Walt?"

"I assume so." She flipped the page. "I can't make out any more. Wait. Here. *My Christmas cowboy kept his promise.*"

"So he made it back."

A burnt odor drew her from the book. Smoke plumed from the pan. "Are you burning something?"

Colt raised a brow at her, and then his nostrils flared and he spun to face the stove. "No."

He grabbed the pan, burning his hand and dropping the hot pan to the floor. She set the book to the side and raced to help him. Grabbing the towel, she lifted the pan and set it in the sink then turned on the water and guided his hand under it.

"I thought I was the bad cook." She studied his hand, but it didn't look bad. "You alright?"

His lips twitched. "Better than dinner, I'm afraid."

She shrugged. "Peanut butter and banana sandwiches work for me."

"That sounds gross."

"Don't knock it until you try it." She got out the ingredients and slapped some peanut butter on some bread and sliced bananas while he cleaned up the floor. It felt good to know more about the McKinnie sisters. Although she still hadn't found out much about her mother, she understood where she'd come from. But she still didn't know much about the man in her kitchen. "You owe me."

He dried the pan and then stepped back, eyeing her. "I'm sure I do, but in what way?"

"You promised to share your story. It's your turn to have your deepest and most scarring secrets cut open and bled out in front of me."

He brushed past her, warming her faster than the burning wood in front of her. "Right. That."

He set the pan in the cabinet. "You already know that my father disowned me, and now I'm not sure what I want to do with the rest of my life. I've never lived up to his expectations, unlike my brother. I'm the oldest, so I should've wanted to be him, but I've never liked his life. I want my own life."

She leaned against the wall, worried that if she moved, he might stop talking. And she wanted to know as much about him as he knew about her. Not to even the playing field but because she genuinely wanted to know more about this man.

"I worked in the family business, trying to impress my father, but I never managed to get his respect. Not that I deserved it. I tried to make it work, but I was never happy following in his footsteps. I realized I was unhappy. I felt dead inside." He yanked open the refrigerator and took out some milk and poured two glasses. "Last night, despite being trapped in that cabin, I hadn't felt that free in years. Free from judgment, free from mistakes, free from my father." He took in a deep breath and closed his eyes. "I'm not poor. Technically, I am homeless, but I can get money if necessary. I went along with your assumption, but I shouldn't have. I didn't know you then."

She chuckled. "I can't blame you. Not like I gave you a chance to tell the truth with a shotgun in your face."

He took a bite of her proffered sandwich and rewarded her with a smile, but then he opened the refrigerator door and grabbed some vegetables. "Just adding a side dish."

She nodded. "It's refreshing to meet someone who has tried to be something they aren't to make their family happy. I feel like you understand me in a way no one else can. I'm so tired of the liars of this world who pretend to be something they're not, just to get what they want. There is nothing worse than a user."

Saige settled on the barstool and watched him cook with passion. Chopping vegetables like an artist creating a masterpiece, sniffing spices, and all the time smiling. "Maybe you could be a chef," she chimed out, way too lighthearted for a man pouring his heart out to her.

Mid-chop, his knife stopped, as if he was contemplating her comment.

"All I'm saying is that you're young, smart, talented, brave, handsome, and a good cook. Why do you have to return to something you don't love? Find what you want to do with the rest of your life."

"Like you?" He tossed vegetables into the frying pan. The aroma of onions and garlic sizzled to life.

The idea of her being free from all obligations of her father's world tempted her to consider his words, but that wasn't reality. "I'm only off for the season. I fought way too hard for way too long to prove myself worthy of more than being Daddy's little girl in the office. I'm only here on break to figure out how to reconnect with my McKinnie side. I need to find balance." She went to the bar, found a bottle of red wine, and opened it, pouring some into two glasses and handing him one.

She took a sip of wine. "What about food critic?"

"Nope. I don't like criticizing other people for doing their job the best they can. Doesn't seem right." He plated the food and grated some parmesan cheese on top before passing it to her.

"Then what do you think you want to be?"

He slid some vegetables onto his plate and poured some sort of lemon butter sauce over it, grabbed his glass, and headed for the table, where he pulled out her chair for her. "I want to be a cowboy."

The way he said it made her snicker, but when his spark faded, she realized he was serious. "Isn't that a song?"

"Yeah, I think it is, but it doesn't make it any less true. I've loved the outdoors since I was young. That and working with my hands. I used to build model planes, and I renovated several rooms in my father's house before I was old enough to head off to college. In college, I took on a job renovating an old mansion as a side job." He let out a quick breath. "My father had no idea. He would've never approved since he only saw my future his way."

"You should be proud of yourself for being brave enough to leave and figure out what you want for yourself. If you want to be a cowboy, then be the best cowboy you can. I was a coward. I ran away from this place because of the loss I couldn't face. I turned to stone and took it out on everyone around me. I was heartless and ruthless in business."

"You don't give yourself enough credit." That sexy grin appeared, so Saige took another few gulps of wine. "You're not either of those things. I'll tell you the type of person who should be ashamed of themselves. It's those people with their lives handed to them by their parents and they waste it on booze and women. I mean, I saw so many of my friends party their parents' money away and never made anything of themselves. Those are the type of people I can't respect."

She dug into her food. Delicious didn't begin to describe the hearty and rich flavors of her meal. Paprika, salt, and pepper tickled her tongue. "Who are you?" she blurted.

"Someone not deserving of you." He took a bite, but she caught a hint of his honesty. Did he really feel that way? She was the unworthy one.

"You're a cultured, well-spoken, kind protector who can cook and wants to be a cowboy. That's a unique combination of traits."

He scooped up the last of his vegetables and dabbed at his mouth before answering. "Thanks, but not sure I buy all that. However, I enjoy renovating and building, and I believe I can help you restore this ranch to its original glory. I need a project to focus on for a while."

She cleared her plate and leaned over the sink, having a mental war with herself. In one breath, she wanted to be his project. In the next, she wanted to send him far away before she found herself in a situation she didn't want to be in ever again.

Something whispered in her ear that there was more to his story that he still held back. Maybe it was her fear of opening her heart, or he was too good to be true, but she knew danger waited ahead. "I didn't come here to find a man. I came to figure out what was broken inside me. To become a woman my mother would be proud of, not disappointed in because of the choices I've made."

His hands rested on her shoulders, offering comfort she didn't deserve, not when she'd been heartless and ruthless for so long to everyone around her. "You had something traumatic happen when you were young. I'm sure your mother would be proud of you for facing it now. Opening your heart to possibilities."

"Possibilities. There's that word again." She turned in his arms, face-to-face, his warm breath sliding over her cheeks. His eyes offered an escape from her sorrow and his words a promise of something better than the life she'd lived. A zing of desire infiltrated her resolve and coaxed her forward, lips parted.

He leaned forward, pressed a kiss to her forehead, and whispered, "When you're ready, I'll be here."

Chapter Twenty-One

IT TOOK everything Colt had not to sweep Saige into his arms and carry her to bed. But she wasn't a one-night woman. She was an every-night dream. Every muscle in his body screamed for him to remain at her side, to take her in his arms and kiss her like no man had ever kissed her before.

He needed to confess he was the playboy who lived off his father's money, but he wanted to show her he was reformed, that she'd reformed him, before he confessed. But he couldn't find the words.

A howl in the distance broke him from his thoughts so he poured another glass of wine for them both. "Let's watch the snow fall by the fire. Now that we have warm bodies and food in our stomachs, it should be a pleasant evening." He settled on the floor next to the stone hearth facing the large glass doors. "First thing I'd suggest is that we build a back deck."

She joined him, to his pleasure, and settled in by his side. "What happened to the deck?"

"Not sure, but it's gone."

"Gone?" She shot up and went to the doors, eyeing outside

as if she'd be able to see beneath the pile of snow. "Seriously? I'm going to murder my cousin." With a head shake and pressed lips, she returned to her seat. "Can't believe I've been paying him all these years to look after the place and he's done nothing. That's what I get for not looking after it myself."

"Stop. No more beating yourself up. Let go of the past."

She lifted her glass. "Fine. To letting go of the past."

They sat on the ground until the wood burned out and the moon hung high in the sky. He knew he needed to tell her now. There was no more procrastinating. "Saige?"

"Mmmhmm?"

He kissed the top of her head and held tight, hoping this wouldn't be the last time he held her. "I need to tell you something, but I need you to let me finish before you react." He took in a deep breath, and when she didn't say anything, he continued. "I want to be the man worthy of you, but there's something in my past I'm not sure you can forgive. I'm the man you can't respect. I'm not poor. I have money. Lots of money. Saige, I'm the billionaire playboy you can't respect." He held his breath, waiting for her response, but the only answer was a soft snore.

COLT DIDN'T WANT to leave since he had Saige curled in his arms on the floor by the fire, sound asleep, but he knew there was one thing he wanted to give her before she sent him away. The Christmas tree from her childhood.

He wasn't sure about the laws of cutting down trees up here, but he was sure no one would ever find out, considering where they were, so he slid out and dressed in his warmest clothes and the new snow boots Saige had bought him. His guilt pinched his heart with the knowledge that she had no clue what he'd done.

He had to do something, anything, to make her feel like there was one man in this world who wanted to make her happy, not miserable. Outside, the wind had died down, but he knew he wouldn't make it far in the deep snow, so he grabbed the axe he'd seen from the garage and went for the tree line closest to the house.

All he found were trees taller than three houses and sprouts, barely taller than a weed poking out of the snow. He trudged deeper in, heaving for air at the effort and the climate. Apparently, running on a treadmill had nothing on walking a few feet with an axe on his shoulder in the winter wilderness.

His efforts were semi-rewarded by a young sapling that would have to do. It wasn't perfect, but it was big enough to put some homemade decorations on and set up in the main room.

With a tight grip on the handle, he swung low and hit his target. The tree spit bark onto the white surface, but barely a notch showed. This would be harder than he'd thought. He swung again and chipped away some more. His shoulders burned by the fourth swing, but in the quiet of the woods, thoughts came rushing in about his life. About what his stepmother had said. Could it be true that his father wanted to give him the space to figure out what he wanted?

Another swing, and a large notch in the wood exposed fresh pine scent. That's when he truly saw what he'd done to the family. He'd told himself he'd done everything he could to be a good son, but he hadn't. In his desire to punish his father for how he'd treated his wife, Colt's mother, he'd caused more damage to his family than his father ever could. After thinking about what his stepmother had said, he knew there was truth to it.

He swung and hit so hard the tree arched at the split, but his shoulders screamed in protest, so he took a break, leaning on the axe and sending out puffs of white air.

If his father had really given him a gift to figure out what he wanted, he'd succeeded. With tight lungs, burning arms, and aching biceps, he'd never felt so good. He turned and eyed the ranch through the trees, and the sight took his breath away. All these years, he'd lived a privileged life that he'd never wanted. Perhaps he had too much of his mother in him. He saw it in that moment. The reason they'd split. His parents were never meant to be together.

During his childhood, his mother had always been sad. She'd mentioned feeling trapped. That life could be a coffin, and no matter how much she scratched and cried out, no one opened it for her to breathe. Not until the divorce. The divorce that sent her to travel the world and leave him behind.

It wasn't his father he'd resented all these years, but his mother. The mother who had left him behind. His chest burned, and tears fought for escape.

In that moment, in the quiet of the mountain, he'd finally stopped working long enough to see it—the truth—and he didn't like it. He wouldn't do to his baby sister what his mother had done to him. The minute he'd been sent away, he'd embraced the escape and didn't want to return, and he guessed his father knew that.

He only hoped he could return with Saige by his side to visit his baby sister, bring her here on holidays to ride horses and see the beautiful snow. This was the world he wanted, but he didn't have to abandon his old life and family to have it. He didn't have to be his mother.

With a deep breath, he hacked away until the tree fell, and then he grabbed hold of the trunk to drag it back to the ranch. The worn-down, broken ranch he hoped to fix up and find a home in. He'd known it at first sight. This place with Saige was what he wanted. Now he had to tell her everything and convince her to trust him. No matter how long it took. He'd work hard to get what he wanted, now that he knew exactly what that was, thanks to his father.

His heart softened to the old man. A man who chose his son over his business. A choice Colt knew had to have crushed him. There had to be a way to help his father and have his own life. Knowing his stepmother, she'd be able to help with that negotiation. Once he made a public apology for what he'd done to his family, he'd be able to move on and figure out what was next. It was time for him to own his mistakes and make them right. To be a man worthy of Saige McKinnie.

He dragged the tree to the house, where he spotted Saige running down the steps to greet him.

"I can't believe you did this," she squealed.

"No berries, but I can make popcorn, and I'm sure we can find something to tie on the end of the branches."

She peppered kisses all over his face, and when he nuzzled her neck and held her in his arms, it wasn't the same explosion of passion but something more. Not pure sexual desire, but a deeper, inexplicable feeling he'd never experienced.

"What are you doing out here in your slippers?" He carried her to the steps, set her softly on her feet, and then dragged the tree up to her.

"Come on. I'll help." She grabbed a limb at the base of the

trunk, and they yanked and pulled until they had it up the stairs.

"We'll make a mess with the needles and snow inside," he warned.

"So, a mess is easy to clean up. Who cares? It's a Christmas tree."

"I can't imagine not caring about a mess in the house." He set the tree up in the main room, leaning into the corner.

Saige rushed into the kitchen and returned with a mug. "Wasn't sure where you were, but I made some coffee in hopes you hadn't disappeared on me."

"There's one thing I'll never do, and that's disappear on you." He took a sip of his coffee, savoring the familiar McKinnie blend, kissed her on the cheek, and made his way to the kitchen.

"What are you doing?" she asked.

"Popping some popcorn." It felt like an elf danced on his excitement button. "I've never decorated a Christmas tree."

"You what? You're not serious." She shook her head.

"I am." He made his way to the kitchen, but she didn't follow.

He heard a creak from upstairs and thought she might have gone into the attic. Colt hoped she remembered where to crawl on the support boards. She returned, box in hand, by the time he finished with the popcorn.

"What's that?"

"We needed sewing supplies to string the popcorn, silly, and a stand to put the tree in." She winked, playful, light, happy. He loved this Saige.

Love was a strong word for a person he'd only known a short time. His stepmother had once told him that all it took was a look, and her and his father's lives changed in an instant. Colt never understood how she thought that was okay when it destroyed a marriage, but now he saw the truth. His mother and father's marriage was destroyed the day they said I do.

He positioned the tree in the stand, and Saige filled it with water, and then they sat on the couch, her legs in his lap while she threaded a needle and he passed her popcorn that she slid onto the string. He picked up another one and tossed it into her mouth, and they both laughed.

The fire crackled, the sun shone bright, and he never thought he could ever feel this complete again. They were a team, a team of two that strung popcorn and wrapped it around the tree then cut strips of red cloth and tied them in bows at the end of the branches.

"Apparently, they used to have candles on the trees, but that tradition ended after a fire one year. I don't know all the details, but after that, they tied bows." She shrugged.

When the last bow was tied, they stood back and eyed their simply decorated Christmas tree. It leaned to one side and had a bare spot here and there, but it was the most magical tree he'd ever seen because he'd decorated it with Saige.

With no more time to waste, he turned her to face him. "Saige, I need to tell you something."

"Shh." She put a finger to his lips, and her eyes blazed.

He wanted—needed—to tell her everything, but apparently, he wasn't the evolved man he thought he was, because when she moved closer, he lost all thoughts and embraced her with all the lust he'd been holding back for weeks.

SAIGE STOOD on her toes and wrapped her arms around his neck, surrendering to her desire, and she wasn't disappointed. Because any kiss from her past faded away, overshadowed by this toe-curling, body-heating, heart-pounding embrace.

At the moment she thought about pulling back and putting the brakes on, he wrapped his arms around her and lifted her tight against him. His heart pounded fast and hard against her chest, and she clutched him like he was the only flicker of heat in a blizzard.

He slowed the passionate pace into a waltz and then lowered her to the ground with a nibble on her lip, resting his forehead to hers with his eyes closed. "Wow."

"I agree," she whispered.

He panted and heaved like he'd lost his breath completely. He let her go but didn't move away, only pressed his palms to the wall above her head. "I hope you don't ever regret that."

She tugged his bottom lip down with her thumb and did a little nibbling of her own. He groaned and pushed from the wall, his hands behind his head. "I need to tell you something."

A warning flare went off, but she wouldn't go there. "Go ahead. I'm listening." She slid her arms around his waist from behind and rested her cheek against his back, listening to his heart pound.

But a knock at the front door pounded louder. "Hey, you okay in there?" Trevor's voice echoed through the house and sliced through her moment.

She must've been so caught up in that life-altering kiss she hadn't heard the truck roll up her drive. Agitation pooled in the pit of her stomach, so she released Colt to tell Trevor to get lost for good. He had no power over her anymore.

No matter, she'd send him away and never think about him

again, because she felt it, her heart mending each day she had Colt in her life.

With her shoulders back, ready to face any battle, she swung open the door but didn't see Trevor's face, only a printed copy of an article with the headline: *Billionaire Bad Boy Colt Whitmore cares more about partying and womanizing than running his father's global empire. A man born with a silver Mercedes in his mouth is caught with sheik's wife in his arms.*

Chapter Twenty-Two

SAIGE'S cold stare shivered Colt from skull to toes. How could the mood switch in the time it took to strike a match? Trevor had struck the match that set Colt's lies on fire. He reached out with both hands to catch her before she could run from him, in fear he'd never catch her again.

Trevor bolted in between them and smacked the paper to his chest. "Time for you to go. We don't need your kind 'round here. We take care of our own."

"The way you took care of her the day her mother died?" Colt fisted his hands, wanting to swing and put the guy on his backside where he belonged.

Trevor smiled, the kind that warned he had a counter to his comment. "You mean a decade ago when I sacrificed our relationship, the woman I loved, because her father told me she was so broken the only hope would be to get her away from this town until she recovered from her depression?"

"What?" she asked in a weak voice.

Trevor turned and dared to touch her arm, but she slipped from his attentions. "Your father told me I had to send you away or you were going to end your life the way your aunt had. That you were depressed. I was so destroyed, and I knew I wasn't strong enough to let you go, but when I saw you at your mother's funeral, I knew it was true—you'd end your life if you didn't find some sort of happiness."

"You're trying to tell her that you slept with another woman for her sake? She's not some young girl. She's too smart to listen to this garbage."

"Stop. Both of you. Stop." She pressed her hands to her ears, and tears flowed down her face. "I can't believe this. I fell for more lies. Men are incapable of being honest."

She dropped her hands to her sides. "Get out."

Trevor moved in, and Colt raised his fists, ready to strike. "You heard the lady. She wants you to leave."

"Both of you!" she yelled. Her voice cracked, and she backed away. "I'm done with you both. Get out."

"Saige," Colt begged.

She strummed the bracelet but then looked down, the cowboy hat no longer hanging from it. "No, no, no. This isn't happening."

Colt didn't care what she'd said or about Trevor's challenge. He pushed him aside to reach Saige. "I'll help you find it. Maybe by the tree."

He rushed to the main room where they'd shared several nights in each other's arms. Would he ever have that again? He'd been so stupid.

Saige joined him, tearing apart the room while Trevor stood in the entryway watching them. "What's that thing?" He pointed at the tree in the corner.

"A family Christmas tree," Colt announced as if to insinuate that he and Saige were together. He picked up the blankets and the pillows and got down on his hands and knees, fumbling around under the couch and chairs.

"It's not here." She ran to the kitchen with Colt at her heels.

"Where did you see it last?" Colt asked.

She shook her head. "Don't know."

"You had it in town because you were toying with it the way you do when something makes you uncomfortable," Colt offered.

She eyed Trevor, and he knew that was what had set her off back in town. Colt tried to keep her attention on him, stepping in between them. "And you had it at the cabin."

Trevor marched into the kitchen. "I can look at the cabin for it."

"No, I had it when we walked out the door. I shut the door and adjusted my gloves and saw the charm then."

"If you lost it outside, you'll never find it." Trevor removed his hat and held it in his hands.

His words obviously pierced Saige, causing her to hold her heart.

"I'll find it," Colt said.

"You can't find a little charm in all that snow." Trevor laughed, his belly-deep mockery echoing through the ranch.

"I can try."

"No." Saige slumped against the counter. "Trevor's right."

The guy grew two inches of pure attitude. "You can leave now. I'll give you a ride into town." Trevor wedged himself between Colt and Saige. "Then I'll come back. We can talk."

"I don't think Saige wants to speak to you," Colt said in a low growl, but he didn't wait for a response. He hotfooted it to the front door and down the front steps, where he dropped down to his knees and dug in the snow.

Trevor showed up but remained on the porch with arms crossed, watching his manic hand shoveling.

"You're a fool. Down on your knees looking for some trinket for a woman." Trevor shook his head.

Colt clawed and clawed and clawed, but out of breath, he sat back on his heels, realizing it had to be on that hill. He'd search for the charm until he found it or died trying. And then after that, he'd figure out how to be the man Saige deserved. He'd start with a public apology to his family, because he saw the damage he'd done, thanks to Saige. He only hoped someday she'd forgive him, or, at the very least, find someone truly worthy of her love.

The front door opened and out stepped Saige. He saw it, her armor put back on to protect her heart. She dropped his bag on the ground and looked at him with no emotion in her eyes as she spoke softly. "I've packed for you."

SAIGE SAT on the floor by the fireplace with no flames, crying. She'd cried all the tears she'd held in for ten years and then some. Her eyes stung, her throat was tight, and her head throbbed.

Not even the pounding on the front door drew her to move.

"I brought your car back," Trevor shouted through the door, but she didn't answer again, like the other times he'd come by in the last three days.

"You need to come out of this house at some point. I'll leave your keys on the porch. If I don't see you in town tomorrow, or if you don't answer this door, I'll break it down."

She didn't doubt his threat. Trevor had never had patience. Why she'd ever fallen for him beyond the fact she'd been young and stupid, she wasn't sure. The trash he spoke about sleeping with another woman to let her go almost made her laugh. How naive did he think she still was?

She couldn't remain on the floor for the rest of her life. Part of her wanted to find Colt and give him a chance to explain. Another part wanted to keep all men from her life forever.

The chilly, dark, and lonely house felt empty without Colt. The way he'd kissed her in the cabin toyed with her determination to keep him out of her life. Where was he now? Trevor had returned every day, but not one knock from Colt to beg her forgiveness.

She pushed herself up and eyed the Christmas tree. The idea of what the holiday would've been like teased her resolve, but what would one faux family tradition mean long term? This wasn't real. It was fantasy. She'd wanted to have what her great-grandmother Francine had back in the 1870s. That darn diary had almost made her believe that a man could really be that dependable and loving.

She picked up Francine's diary and threw it against the wall. "Legends and lies!"

The book slammed against the wall and popped open, a piece of paper falling from the pages. Saige dropped to her knees and eyed her name written in her mother's script.

Her mouth went death dry. With trembling hands, she picked it up, opening it to find a note addressed to her.

MY SWEET SAIGE,

I'm sorry I'm leaving you so soon. You are my joy, my every-

thing. I'm afraid I need you to find that inner McKinnie strength, because he'll need you. The man who used to be all purrs and passion has turned cold and broken. He's always been a giving and loving man, and I never thought he'd ever turn his heart away from the world, but I'm afraid my diagnosis has crushed him. I fear he won't be the father you deserve, but he loves you so much, he can't face another loss. I've pleaded with him to be by your side, to teach and love you the way we wanted to do together. I'm afraid his bitterness may get in the way, but I know my sweet baby girl will show him how to open his heart again once I'm gone.

Take the cowboy charm and hold it tight. Remember what it represents. It is love, honor, compassion, and love. All the things I know you to be and wish for you.

I'll be watching you from heaven and sending snow kisses with each flake that touches your cheeks.

Love,
Mom

SAIGE EYED the picture of her mother she'd held all night, wishing she could hear her sing again, or that her mother could kiss her goodnight and tuck her into bed, or tell her what to do when her heart ached for a man who'd lied to her, despite knowing her truth.

Because if he would've told her he was like Trevor, she would've ended things that moment and sent him packing. Then she could've avoided the drama.

She placed her mother's picture on the hallway table and vowed, "I'm going to restore our home and figure out how to make sure it remains a place for families to enjoy horses and hiking and all the things we once did together. Even if I can't have a family, I can make this place for others to enjoy."

With heavy feet, she managed to go upstairs, shower, dress, and make her way to town to find a contractor to hire to do the work.

With no real snow in the last few days, she managed to get to town with no issue. When she passed where her car had gone into the embankment, she slowed, eyeing where they'd held on to each other to make it up the hill. She remembered how Colt had supported her and held her tight, never wavering by her side.

She shook off the thoughts and made her way into town. She parked and decided to head into the diner, where many of the men hung out before they went to work. Inside, she spotted Mindy, who waved her over. "Hey, look. It's your man."

Saige scanned the restaurant, her pulse skipping, but she didn't see Colt.

"No, silly, not in here. On the TV." Mindy pointed to the television on a shelf high up in the corner, where Colt sat, dressed in a suit, his hair still a little long the way she liked it.

"Turn it up," she said.

The ticker at the bottom of the screen shot by, but all it had was stock info and news headlines. White lines multiplied on the screen, and the sound increased.

"I want to apologize to my family for my behavior and to all those I've harmed in my past for my destructive behavior."

The reporter did that fake concerned yet judgmental face. "Then why did you do it?"

"I thought at the time that I was justified." He tapped his knee and eyed the reporter then looked straight at the camera. "Because I thought that if I punished my father enough, I'd feel better, but he wasn't the one who'd hurt me. There's really no excuse for my behavior. The paper reported the truth. I was a playboy billionaire who acted like a spoiled child, but I want to be a man deserving of respect. I know I have a long way to go to earn it."

"And how will you do that? Will you take your place at your father's side? You're going back to having your bills paid while you jet set around the world?"

"No," Colt chuckled, that deep, sexy sound. Oh, how she'd missed that sound. "I'm saying that I'll be working hard to make my own dreams come true. I won't do that with my father's money. I'm going to start my own business based on my goals and earn the right to call myself a Whitmore. Someday, maybe we'll join forces, but for now, I need to be my own man. A man worthy of the name."

"What about the Billionaire Bad Boys Club tabloids said you joined?" the reporter asked, digging deeper.

"Not my kind of crowd anymore. Besides, from this moment forward, I'm working on being a better man. A man worthy of being trusted and loved."

"That must've been some snowstorm you were trapped in if you reached this revelation. Did you do it on your own, or did you have help? Did you run from the sheik's wife into the arms of another woman? Another conquest?"

"No. I ran to figure out who I am. And I'm a man who won't answer slanderous and misleading questions. From now on, I'm only going to tolerate honesty. I believe everyone deserves that."

Mindy turned down the volume. "You know, I heard he searched that hill for twelve hours that first day for your charm. He only left when the sheriff threatened to put him in a cell after Trevor reported a stranger lurking around his hunting cabin."

Saige closed her eyes, her head spinning. Could Colt really mean what he said? Did he truly understand what he'd done wrong and strive to be a better man?

Saige spotted Trevor's hat before he rounded the wall in her view from the other side of the diner. "Glad you've made it out here. Now, maybe we can talk about us."

"There is no us," she said without wasting another thought on him.

Trevor ran his fingers down her arm. Even through her coat, the touch felt like a curse. "Come on, we were always good together. Besides, I told you I'd help you restore your ranch, and then we can talk about what's next."

"What would be next?" Saige asked.

Mindy tapped her pen on the counter. "Convincing you to invest in his next failed business venture. To marry him so he can take all your money."

"Shut up, Mind. Don't listen to her. She's bitter."

"I'd have to care to be bitter." Mindy grabbed her pad of paper and disappeared into the kitchen, leaving Saige standing in the diner facing Trevor.

"She's upset because we dated for a minute, but don't worry, I'll never even look at another woman again."

"Is that true?" Saige asked but held up a hand to stop him from saying another word. "Don't bother. I don't want to hear anything else because all you do is lie. You lied then, and you're lying to me now."

"You think that man's going to come back for you? He's a billionaire. There's no way he's going to return. That's all fluff, damage control for his father's company. You've always had your head in the clouds and believed in all that sappy romance garbage. That McKinnie mail-order brides legend is the lie here."

She needed to call Colt and see if he would come back. Trevor had a point, though. Why would a billionaire want to return to Rocky Ridge? "Maybe I want to believe in something again. To be like my mother was at the ranch before she got sick. Happy and loving and full of life. I remember how much my father loved her, and it wasn't until she became ill and he lost her that he changed. We both changed. Our hearts shattered, but one person has taken the time to help put mine back together."

Mindy rushed to the door and swung it open. The bell jingled as if to warn about the cold air rushing in. "Oh my goodness, come see this." She waved Saige to the door, so she brushed past Trevor and exited the diner to find a man on a horse trotting up the main street. She couldn't see him because his hat was too low.

Trevor bolted in front of her with fists tight at his side.

The horse slowed until it came to a stop a few feet away, and then the rider looked up, showing Colt's gorgeous face. He slung his leg over and landed like a pro in the street. He cuddled the horse to his chest and pet his muzzle before he tipped his hat up and passed the reins to Mindy. "Can you take him for a minute?"

Mindy only nodded.

Trevor spun and faced Saige. "You're a fool."

"I think you're the fool," Colt's voice sang like Christmas Eve carolers, bringing joy to Saige's heart.

Her mind whirled with thoughts, and her breath came ragged and wild. "You were on TV... I just saw you."

"It was recorded." He held his cowboy hat in his hand, but he wore the boots she'd bought him. "You heard it?"

"You need to leave town. You're not welcome here," Trevor ordered, but Colt didn't budge. "I'll get the sheriff again."

"And I can tell him how you're the one who set fire to his barn in high school," Saige threatened.

Trevor took a step back. His face showed shock, then anger, then fear. "No amount of money in the world is worth dealing with you again. Too perfect all the time. No man can live up to your expectations, ever." He glared at Colt. "You can have her. Good luck."

The past stormed off while she saw her future step in. But could she truly take a chance on a man who'd lied and manipulated her? She retreated from him, needing to think. Her legs were weak and her knees threatened to give way, so she backed into the diner wall.

"I know you don't want to see me, and I'll leave the minute I'm done, but I just needed to give you something."

She looked up to see him down on one knee. "I'm afraid I couldn't find your charm, and this won't be the same, but I had a new one crafted for you. It's a boot with M and W for our last names."

Her heart ached and filled with joy all at the same time. She'd lost her family heirloom but gained a symbol of something new. Of hope. She held out her shaking hands.

"I hope this charm will make you believe in love again. Believe in a man who will treat you like royalty, spend evenings by the fire talking about family traditions, cherish every moment with you, cook for you, and never lie to you again." He clipped the charm onto the bracelet and stood up. "I hope someday I can be your Christmas cowboy." He turned away, but she couldn't do it. She couldn't let him go. Like her mother, she wanted a family at the ranch with the man she loved.

"You forgot something."

"What's that?" he asked with soft eyes and a humble tilt of his head.

"A heart-pounding, feel-it-to-my-toes amazing kiss."

His mouth turned up into a mischievous grin. "I'd count myself lucky, ma'am."

She threw her arms around him and surrendered to possibilities. The possibility of true love with her own Christmas cowboy.

Epilogue

Two Years Later

Colt waited by the Christmas tree with such joy in his heart, he thought he could fly to heaven and meet Saige's mom in person. The sound of Saige hanging up the phone—that he'd had fixed before agreeing to allow her to be here for even five minutes without him—drove him to open his arms and pull her into his side. "What did he say?"

"Dad says he'll be here on Friday. He also said he is bringing my mother's book she created, retelling what was in the diary. I can't wait to find out what happened between my relatives all those years ago."

Colt placed a hand on her swollen belly and felt his little man kick. The idea of a baby, his baby, brought him so much joy, he thought he'd burst. "My baby sister and my father and stepmother will be here Friday. And any day now, we'll meet my little man, Turner."

"Or girl, Tammie," she reminded him.

"Well, we better finish up the Christmas decorations." Colton urged, knowing he wanted to hurry so they could resume their position by the fire, since each year they'd sleep out here in memory of their first week together.

"One thing first. I want to go grab my grandmother's diary. I think it's in the Christmas box where we left it two years ago."

"I'm glad we came home for Christmas this year." Colt let Saige go, but only because it meant she'd get back all that more quickly.

"I love that you call it home." Saige went to the room, brought back the Christmas box, and dug in.

"Oh my goodness!" she squealed, startling Colt to her side.

"Are you okay? Baby okay?"

"Better than okay. Look." She held up the old Christmas charm. "It must've fallen off when we decorated the tree before everything happened."

"I can't believe it's been here all this time." Colt took the charm and strung it on her bracelet.

"I'm so sorry. I know you never gave up searching for it."

He kissed her hand. "I'm just glad you found it. Now we can pass it down to our little girl and tell her our story. Except maybe leave out the part where Daddy was hungover and Mom pulled a shotgun on him."

"But that would be a lie," she said with a wink.

He knelt down, pressed his ear to her belly, and wrapped his arms around Saige. "I can promise I'll never lie to our baby unless she meets a guy like Trevor, and then I'll say whatever I need to, and I'm borrowing your shotgun."

They both settled in front of the roaring fire with hot cocoa and snuggled up together in the McKinnie ranch.

That Christmas Eve, a new McKinnie-Whitmore baby was

born. In keeping with the long family tradition, the precious little girl was named Teagan Rosemary McKinnie-Whitmore.

The End

If you enjoyed this book please consider checking out the McKinnie Mail Order Brides series with Love on the Ranch.

Irish Whiskey Cake

Ingredients:

Cake

- 1 *18 ounce) box yellow cake mix
- 1 box instant vanilla pudding (3.5 oz)
- 4 eggs
- 1/2 cup oil
- 1 cup whole or 2% milk
- 1 1/2 oz whiskey
- 1 cup pecans or walnuts, chopped

Icing

- 1/2 cup melted butter
- 1 cup sugar
- 1/2 cup whiskey

Directions:

Cake

1. Preheat oven to 350 degrees F
2. Combine all ingreidents and mix by hand for 3-4 minutes
3. Pour into well greased bundt pan and bake 50-60 minutes
4. Test with a toothpick. If it comes out clean then cake is done.

Icing

1. Cook over medium heat on stovetop
2. place all ingredients into sauce pan and cook until the sugar is dissolved and liquid is brown
3. Leave cake in bundt pan, poke several holes into cake with toothpick
4. Pour 3/4 of icing onto cake.
5. Wait 15 minutes and then flip cake over onto plate.
6. Brush remaining icing on top and sides of cake

Reader's Guide

1. How many of you have read the McKinnie Mail Order Bride series? If so, did you feel connected to this story at the start due to Saige being a descendant of the original sisters? If not, do you have a desire to go back and read about her great, great, great, great grandmother?

2. Do you think Colt should've told Saige the truth immediately about who he was? If so, do you think she would've sent him away immediately?

3. Do you think Saige found what she was looking for when she returned to her family ranch?

4. Could you ever return to the town after what Saige had been through with her ex and the death of her mother and her father turning his heart cold?

5. Do you think Saige's father buried his pain in work? If he hand't, do you think Saige would've returned to the ranch to seek out a connection with her mother?

6. Have you ever wanted to love someone because they are perfect on paper and exactly who you thought you wanted but there was no chemistry?

7. Do you think that in the future Colt and Saige will spend more time in the city or at the ranch? Why?

8. If you were Saige, would you forgive Colt's lies and welcome him back into your life?

9. Why do you think Trevor cheated on Saige the day of her mother's funeral? Do you think he was telling the truth or spinning more lies when he told her why he did that to her?

10. Would you want to read more books about the ranch or the McKinnie family?

Also by Ciara Knight

For a complete list of my books, please visit my website at www. ciaraknight.com. A great way to keep up to date on all releases, sales and prizes subscribe to my Newsletter. I'm extremely sociable, so feel free to chat with me on Facebook, Twitter, or Goodreads.

For your convenience please see my complete title list below, in reading order:

CONTEMPORARY ROMANCE

Friendship Beach Series

Summer Island Book Club

Summer Island Sisters

Summer Island Hope

Summer Island Romance

Sweetwater County Series

Winter in Sweetwater County

Spring in Sweetwater County

Summer in Sweetwater County

Fall in Sweetwater County

Christmas in Sweetwater County

Valentines in Sweet-water County

Fourth of July in Sweetwater County

Thanksgiving in Sweetwater County

Grace in Sweetwater County

Faith in Sweetwater County

Love in Sweetwater County

A Sugar Maple Holiday Novel

(Historical)

If You Keep Me

If You Choose Me

A Sugar Maple Novel

If You Love Me

If You Adore Me

If You Cherish Me

If You Hold Me

If You Kiss Me

Riverbend

In All My Wishes

In All My Years

In All My Dreams

In All My Life

A Christmas Spark

A Miracle Mountain Christmas

HISTORICAL WESTERNS:

About the Author

Ciara Knight is a USA TODAY Bestselling Author, who writes clean and wholesome romance novels set in either modern day small towns or wild historic old west. Born with a huge imagination that usually got her into trouble, Ciara is happy she's found a way to use her powers for good. She loves spending time with her characters and hopes you do, too.